QUINCY

A Wheaten Terrier's Adventure through Life

DIANE MCHUTCHISON

Illustrated by Wendy Carty

Copyright © 2022 Diane McHutchison
All rights reserved
First Edition

NEWMAN SPRINGS PUBLISHING
320 Broad Street
Red Bank, NJ 07701

First originally published by Newman Springs Publishing 2022

ISBN 978-1-68498-467-1 (Paperback)
ISBN 978-1-68498-469-5 (Hardcover)
ISBN 978-1-68498-468-8 (Digital)

Library of Congress Control Number: 2022915463

Printed in the United States of America

To Quincy, whom I shall miss forever

Dogs do speak, but only to those who know how to listen.
—Orhan Pamuk

Contents

Acknowledgements 1

Hi! I'm Quincy 5
A New Home, a New Family 23
School Days 35
A Trip to the Mountains 48
Quincy's First Christmas 57
More Adventures 64
Here's Duffy 69
Ouch! 84
Where Are We Going Now? 97
Snacks and Goodies and Treats, Oh My! 113
A Dog Named Kitty? 121
Mom's Hurt 132
Duffy's Sick 139
Welcome, Alvin! 146
Adventures with Alvin 155
Saying Goodbye 161
New Friends and Feathers 178

Author's Note 182

Acknowledgements

Thank you, John, my husband, for your unwavering support in all my endeavors. I know you always have my back and that the dogs will be well cared for while I'm distracted by books, yarn, or glass.

This never could have been accomplished without the Wheatens 3, then the Wheatens 2.5, and now the Wheatens 2. Quincy, our perfect gentleman and thoughtful Zen puppy; Duffy our linebacker and clown; Ciara, the little twerking hussy; and finally Aoidhghean, who has more swagger than a ship full of pirates—you have given me more than enough material to write three more books!

To our friends (and their pups) who were instrumental in getting this written, without y'all, and your particular means of encouragement, this would still be just a thought:

- Barbara (Madison)—Your friendship through all these years has been a lifeline. You are definitely one in a million! Our weekly game nights allowed my mind to work through sticky bits through distraction.
- Kate (Smudge)—Your encouragement and support has been more valuable to me than you'll ever realize. Best damn saw I ever bought.
- Deb—I have struggled to come up with an appropriate comment to summarize your support. I've given up… and I'll just say that your support and friendship mean the world to me.
- Dr. Barbara, VMD—Our favorite vet who has guided us gently from puppy to senior, thank you for saving Quincy's

life (and mine!) that fateful November evening and for the outstanding care you've given our entire pack.
- Jan—Baker extraordinaire! The goodies fueled late-night writing sessions.
- Annamarie and Tom—I am so glad that Ann and I "stayed on the bus" all those years ago and allowed our friendship to grow. Your encouragement kept me going.
- Jack and Donna and Paul and Robin—Thank you for being great neighbors, especially as our pack has run up and down along the fence line, barking like little furry fools.
- Vicki (Moose and others)—Our pet sitter without equal, you enabled an escape from the house so vital for John and me!
- Barbara and Stephen ("Theologian" Riley)—You were the first "Facebook wheaten people" we met in real life, and our lives are richer for it.
- Gregg and Melissa—The best biscuit makers on the planet, you keep the pups happy, even finicky Quincy.

To our friends who own (or were owned by) wheatens (and a few other critters), any similarity in name, behavior, or ownership just might have been intentional, or accidental, or modified to make things easier to read. (Think Alvin instead of Aoidhghean.) You made this possible because of your stories and videos—inspiration!

- Toni (Rosa, Peaches, and others); Frank and Gaye (Erin); San and Malcom (Ruffle and others…and they do live in faraway England); Diane, Rob, and the soon-to-be Dr. Armen, DVM (Danny, Marnie, and Breslin); Sherry and Mike (Bailey and Sulley); Pat (Murphy, Reilly, and Mochi); Denise (Molly June, Sunny, Charles, Bubis, Lilly Rose, and a few more); Jerri (Bailey, Bentley, and Tagalong); Camilla (Bacchus); Michelle (Riley and Dallas); Lisa (Morgayne, Seamus, Rusty, Finnegan, and others); Laura (Sophie, Winston, and Whitney); Jeanne (Whiskey, Sprocket, Mr. Bear, and others); Pam and Stephan (Jada); Catherine and

Mark (AJ, Henry, Igor, Squish, and a few others); Winona (Aussie), Caroline (Gracie, Lilly, and Monet); Maggie (Argyle Jasper, Mazie, and Edna); Roy (Charm and JB); James (Ruby and Lucy); and Diane (Abigail Snottycat)

Finally, but certainly not the least, to the wheaten terrier community, we all share a love of this wonderful breed; and I thank you all for welcoming us into your pack.

Oh, if it appears as though I forgot someone, it truly wasn't intentional. You haven't seen my desk. I know your name is on a scrap of paper somewhere.

Hi! I'm Quincy

Hi! I'm Quincy. I'm an Irish soft-coated wheaten terrier. When I was born, I lived with one human, Camilla; my mom, Morgan; and my puppy brothers and sisters. My dog dad, Ruffle, lived with his human parents, San and Malcom, in faraway England. My dog dad came to the United States for a dog show and met my mom while here in the United States.

My brothers are named Sulley, Murphy, Whiskey, and Danny. My sisters are Molly June and Sophie. We had lots of fun playing together. We liked to play different games, and then we snuggled together for naps. Morgan watched over us closely and made sure that we learned our puppy lessons.

I don't remember much from my first two weeks. I mostly wanted to sleep and eat, especially since my eyes had not opened yet. Dogs are different from people in a lot of ways. One of the big differences is that our eyes do not open right after we are born. That didn't slow any of us in finding our food, and we snuggled together for our naps so that we could know where everyone is. It was very comforting to listen to everyone as they softly snored. Every now and then, someone would kick someone else, but that was usually to get more space. Mom kept a close eye to make sure that no one got hurt and that we all got plenty to eat.

When I was about a week and a half old, I noticed a tiny light. Curious, I tried to crawl toward the light and bumped into my brother Danny. He told me that his eyes were completely open and that the world looked to be an amazing place! He was excited to tell me everything, and his enthusiasm was catching. He said that we each had a ribbon around our necks and the ribbons were all distinct colors. He guessed that was so that Cam could tell us apart. Mom didn't have that problem—she could tell us apart by smelling us. Danny went on to tell me that we were in a special puppy area, with all seven of us together with our mom. He said that the walls would keep us in the area, but Mom could step over them. Danny wondered out loud what was beyond the walls.

Before I go any further, I guess I should explain that dogs, like people, sometimes have two names. Our human mom, Camilla, is called Cam by nearly everyone. All the puppies in our litter have our registered name and a call name. The registered name is used on our official paperwork, and our call name is what is used every day. Registered names always include the kennel name so that everyone knows where we were born. Our kennel is Bacchus Wheatens. As a result, my registered name is Bacchus To Dream the Impossible Dream. Sulley's registered name is Bacchus It's Summertime and the Living is Easy. Molly June's registered name is Bacchus My Fair Lady. Breeders often use a theme for their litters, and ours is famous songs from Broadway shows. Those names are too long for everyday use, of course, so we have shorter everyday names. In the beginning, before we were given our call names, Cam kept track of us by the color of ribbon we each wore. We didn't get our call names until we went to live with our forever homes. I'm using everyone's call names in my story, though, to make it easier to keep track of everyone.

Anyway, over the next day or so, everyone's eyes opened. We excitedly squeaked to one another as we spotted new things to point out to each other. We also started to wander around in our puppy area a bit more. Mom would pick us up and gently move us if we started to get too far away from her. Danny really kept her busy! He was always trying to get to the other side of the walls.

Mom showed us the soft blankets that Cam had put down for us to nap on, and she laughed softly as we tried to walk on the slippery tile floor. Cam kept a close eye on us; and after we had our meals, she would pick us up by the scruff of our neck, just like Morgan would, and then gently put us down on some crinkly paper. She would tell us, "Go potty," as she gently set us down on the paper. Over the next few days, I figured out what she meant and tried to get to the crinkly paper whenever I needed to go to the bathroom. I didn't always get there in time, but I tried. I was extremely excited when Cam noticed what I was doing, and she gave me an extra treat! She called me a "good boy" as she gave me the little piece of cheese.

I told the others about my discovery. Whiskey was the first to try it out; and he, too, got the little piece of cheese. Sophie was next and was also rewarded with a bit of cheese. Sulley and Danny listened to me. But neither were particularly interested in the cheese, so they didn't rush to the crinkly paper. Molly June would wander over to get the cheese. But she wasn't doing the potty thing, so she didn't get any. She walked over to our mom to pout and complain. Mom just laughed at Molly June and reminded her that treats were rewards. Molly grumbled her disagreement.

Just like people, puppies have their own personalities. Cam watched us as we played and grew, and she made mental notes about each of us, knowing that this information would help match us to our forever homes. When I first heard about our "forever homes," I wasn't too sure about the idea of another home other than here; but the way she kept describing it, forever home started to sound pretty exciting. Still I worried about leaving and hoped that we would be able to visit each other once we moved to our forever homes.

One afternoon, I heard Cam talking to someone named Denise on the phone. Cam was laughing as she described Molly June and her treats. Cam explained that, from the first day that she could, Molly would reach out with her paw as a gentle reminder that she would like an extra treat. She had tried to convince Cam that we needed treat stations in every room, but that had not happened yet. I heard Cam laughing as she told Denise that Molly was as stubborn as could be, but then she added, "That's a terrier for you."

Terriers are a determined bunch. We range from short to tall, from Welsh terrier to Airedale terrier. In general, once we are interested in a task, it is difficult to deter us from doing it. Of course, being as smart as we all are, things work most smoothly if we believe the task is our idea in the first place.

During our time with Cam, she made sure that we developed good social skills and that we learned about the world around us.

She gave us the opportunity to play with many different toys and to try out lots of new things. Cam tried to introduce us to a wide range of things so that we could be confident and secure puppies when we went to our new homes. As we explored and experimented, our individual personalities started to blossom and became even more obvious. Cam made sure that we were not frightened by anything that she introduced to us. We didn't have to like everything, but she expected us to try everything.

That expectation was perfectly fine with Murphy. Murphy was the athlete in our family. He was always seeing how fast he could run or how high he could jump. I heard Cam say that Murphy needed a family who would be able to keep him busy. Murphy was too busy trying the balance beam out where the agility toys were to listen to what Cam was saying. Murphy was determined to conquer the agility toys, hoping to please his new family. Making others happy was always his goal.

I liked some of the agility toys, but I wasn't interested in running the full course. In that game, pups are asked to run a path that has the agility toys set up in special places. The toys include high jumps, a balance beam, a teeter-totter, ramps, hoops to jump through, and a tunnel. I didn't mind the ramps and the tunnel, but I was not excited about jumping. I would rather watch everyone else run the agility course.

Cam had a human friend over one day, and they were talking about us. They gently picked each of us up in turn and looked at our teeth. They had us stand on a table and kept putting our feet on some special spots. I understood that they wanted us all to stand exactly the same way, but I wasn't sure why. After a while, I heard them comment that Sophie would show beautifully. I wondered what she would be showing when I heard Cam's friend suggest that Sophie would probably do quite well with Laura, who was experienced with showing dogs. That was when I remembered Mom telling us about dog shows. They could be considered beauty pageants for dogs, and I agreed that my sisters were beautiful and that everyone else would admire them. These dog shows are important because each dog is judged against a formal standard, getting points for being as close as possible to perfect. Once they get enough points, they are called champion. This tells the world that they are great representatives of the breed and should pass along their traits to their own puppies.

Anyway, back to Sophie. Sophie was reserved, but she also liked getting attention. I'm fairly sure that was one of the reasons that Cam thought that she would be a good show dog. Sophie was sort of quiet, and she enjoyed snuggling with someone. She loved taking walks and always held her tail high with pride. Sophie was also very observant. She watched everyone around her and paid special attention to her people. She had a few favorite toys, and she would bring them to Cam when she sensed that Cam was upset. Sophie, like me, also tended to worry; and she confided in me that she was a little concerned about what Cam was thinking about her and what kind of home she would be going to. I assured Sophie that everyone thought that she was a kind and beautiful girl and that she would have the perfect forever home. Sophie thanked me for my confident answer and leaned against me as we settled in for a nap. As I drifted off to sleep, I only wished that I could be as confident as I sounded.

When Sherry called Cam to talk about puppies, Sherry asked specifically about boy puppies. Cam told her about Sulley. Sulley loved water. He was always walking in our water dish or any puddle he found. He enjoyed the little swimming pool that was in the yard but was frustrated that he couldn't really swim in there. I would rather not get wet, but Sulley was happiest playing in the water. Cam said that she hoped to match Sulley with a family who had a swimming pool, and Sherry described their pool. Cam seemed to think that sounded ideal and then went on to mention that she thought he would be a natural for something called dock diving.

I wasn't sure what that was, but I have learned that's a game for dogs where someone throws a toy out into a swimming pool and the pup is asked to run fast and jump far to get the toy. The longest jump wins! I knew that Sulley would excel if he got to try that. Sherry also mentioned that her first wheaten, Bailey, loved riding in their boat and that her new puppy would need to grow into Bailey's life jacket. I thought this made Cam happy, knowing that Sulley would be well taken care of if he went to live with Sherry.

Not all wheaten terriers like water, but we do share many other similar traits. New wheaten owners often are surprised that we tend to sleep in the strangest positions! I liked to sleep on my back, but I usually turned my body so that my feet were against the wall. Cam said that I was holding up the wall. Molly liked to sleep with her body on the floor, using her bed as a pillow. Murphy was happy about that because he would curl up on Molly's bed and then hang his head over the side. I thought they both were silly.

Wheatens also like to do zoomies. Occasionally I would decide that it was the perfect time to run as fast as I could and jump from the couch to the chair to the floor and back again. I would run down the hall and through the kitchen and then back to jumping on the couch and chair. Mom told me that all my brothers and sisters did the same thing, and she even posted a video or two showing my zoomies. According to Sophie's mom, she liked to do zoomies after her bath. Sulley liked to do his zoomies after he got out of the pool. I never had a good excuse for my zoomies other than they were fun.

Wheaten terriers were originally kept on Irish farms to hunt rats and other critters. This helped the farmers because we kept their crops from being destroyed by vermin. This hunting instinct is still in most wheatens, but the need to keep crops safe is not as much of a challenge today. As a result, there are competitions called barn hunts to help keep our hunting skills sharp. In that game, people hide some rats in a maze, and the pup tries to find the rats as quickly as they can. The rats are in plastic cages, so the dogs can only sniff them. They win prizes for speed and accuracy. The rats are never hurt, and in between competitions, they are cared for very well.

Cam had watched Murphy listening for things. She thought that he might enjoy barn hunting. Cam took Murphy out to her barn and see if he had an aptitude for it, and he absolutely loved it. He wasn't afraid to climb up on the bales of hay or crawl through the tunnel that Cam made when she stacked the bales. He quickly learned to sit down to let Cam know that he had found a rat, and Cam was amazed that he ignored the empty cages. When they came back to the house, they were both so excited about how well he had done. Cam gave Patricia a call to tell her that she had found her next barn-hunt champion while Murphy told us his hunts, along with tales about some other animals that he met while out at the barn. He described the cows, goats, and horses that he saw and told us all about their interesting smells. He was almost vibrating with excitement from his day out by the barn.

My brother Danny was the happy-go-lucky clown in our litter. He was willing to just sit and watch everyone, but he would happily join in whatever game someone else was playing. Danny was always the first to the door, wagging his tail to say hi to anyone who came in, and would gently push his way forward to get noticed. He usually wasn't interested in any of the organized games, preferring to just be himself and happy to see everyone. His idea of a perfect afternoon was to be snuggled on the couch next to someone and getting ear rubs and cuddles. He was such a happy and contented pup. Our breed has been described as merry extroverts, and I'm sure that there is a picture of Danny wherever that is written to show everyone just what they mean.

Like my sister Sophie, I was quiet. I didn't want to play the rough-and-tumble games with the others, and I certainly didn't want to get wet with Sulley. I was happiest when I could just sit and watch. I didn't need a lot of attention, but when I wanted to be noticed, I wanted to be noticed. I did have a favorite squeaky toy that I enjoyed playing with. It was a long orange snake, and I enjoyed squeaking it to see how long it would take until I annoyed someone enough that they took it away. I would always get it back, but I liked testing that boundary. Squeak, squeak, squeak, and squeak! Are you annoyed yet? If no one paid attention to me, I'd make it squeak, squeak, and squeak again! When we were outside, I liked to watch and monitor what was going on and bark an alert to everyone if something was out of place. I didn't bark all the time; so when I did bark, everyone knew that it was important, if only important to me. I guess I was the thinker of the group.

As I mentioned, Cam worked hard to introduce us to new things so that we would be confident puppies when we went to our new homes. I've described a few of those things already—barn hunting, swimming, and agility. We also had a lot of time to play and explore on our own. For example, in our puppy play area, we had a whole pile of toys. Many of these were stuffed toys, which we also called stuffies. We played tug, chewed ears off, and happily destroyed a whole bunch of those toys. It became a game, and it was fun to see how quickly we could remove the squeakers or pull out all the fluff. Cam had an endless supply of toys, and we had an endless appetite to destroy them! We kept her on her toes because she had to snatch up the fluff when we ripped open a toy. She was concerned that someone would try to eat the fluff, and that would not have been good at all.

In our play area, Cam had tossed many balls. There were big ones, little ones, squeaky ones, some that rolled funny, and some that had bumps and knobs; and they were all for us! Sometimes Cam or one of her people friends would throw a ball for us to chase. Other times, we played by ourselves. Whiskey liked to carry a ball, drop it, and then give it a push. He would race next to it to see who would win—him or the ball. Murphy liked to find toys hidden in the blankets. If no one else had hidden one, he would hide a few himself, but that wasn't as much fun for him. Sometimes I would help him and hide a toy or a ball. I would run over to him and pretend I was worried that I couldn't find it. He was always excited and happy to help me find it.

Another outdoor game that Cam introduced us to was called lure coursing. In this game, we had to chase a flag attached to a string. A motor pulled the string along, and it was a lot of fun trying to catch that flag! Murphy would start to vibrate with excitement every time Cam brought out that game, and he would start to run after the flag even before Cam had the game completely set up. I really hoped Murphy's new family would be able to keep up with him!

One afternoon, Cam brought in a funny-looking contraption and put it down in our play area. It looked like a cube made from plastic pipes, and a collection of toys hung from the top rung. It didn't take long for a game to begin as Sophie and Danny pushed a toy between them. Molly watched for a minute or two, then tried to take the toy away from them and nearly pulled the entire cube over onto herself. Quick-thinking Murphy grabbed a different toy and pulled the cube back upright. Sophie, Danny, and Murphy turned to Molly to ask what she was thinking when she grabbed that toy. She sheepishly explained that she thought that it might have treats because Sophie and Danny were so interested in it. We had to explain that this was not a new treat station. Of course, Molly was disappointed upon hearing that news.

As the excitement from the new toy station settled down, I noticed that there was a small new platform in our play area. I trotted over to see what it was and, after giving it a thorough sniffing, decided to climb up onto it. Once atop the little platform, I was excited to be able to see over the walls and wondered when, if ever, we would be allowed to explore beyond our puppy area by ourselves. From my vantage point, I could see a hallway that led toward the kitchen and another hallway leading in another direction. I was curious about where that hall led when I found myself pushed off the platform. Danny had noticed the platform and saw me sitting there. He was curious to see what I was looking at but also decided to have a bit of fun at my expense. He clambered up onto the platform and gave me a shove to push me off. While I climbed back on, Danny sat and looked out beyond the walls. I could see that he was thinking something, but I couldn't tell just what.

When I asked him, he just smiled and said, "You'll see."

The next morning, I awoke to some excited yips and squeaks. I looked around and realized that Danny was missing! I ran over to the platform and scrambled onto it to see if I could find him from the higher lookout point.

There he was! Danny was proudly trotting down the hall away from our puppy area, heading toward who knows what! I was so startled that I let out a little bark. It was at that very moment that Cam came around the corner and scooped up Danny and put him back down into our area.

"You're an adventurous puppy, aren't you!" she exclaimed.

We all gathered around Danny to see what stories he could tell. He told us of squishy, fuzzy carpet under his feet as he had trotted down the unknown hallway. But it was pretty dark, and he was hesitant to continue in that direction. That was when he changed his course and headed toward the kitchen. He described the cool hardwood floor and lamented that he had only gotten a glimpse of the kitchen—but that it smelled wonderful. Molly June pushed her way forward, asking if there were treats there. Danny admitted that he didn't know. He hadn't gotten all the way into the kitchen.

A bit later in the afternoon, after our naps, I saw that Cam had made the walls to our area a little bit taller. Clearly excursions were to be discouraged. I really doubted that was going to slow down Danny, and I was right. It did not take Danny long until he figured out how to push the little platform over to the side of our area and then jump over the wall. He had described his plans; so the next thing anyone knew, Murphy, Danny, Whiskey, Sulley, and Molly June had all escaped and were exploring in all different directions.

Mom was trying to pick up her puppies and bring them back into our area, but just as soon as she would get someone back into our area, that pup would escape again and go in a different direction. She finally gave up and gave a warning bark, and I joined her with my own yip, which brought Cam running to see what was going on—puppies everywhere!

Cam tried to be stern with everyone, but we could tell she was laughing at us.

She reached over and gave Sophie and me an extra rub on our ears, saying, "You're the good puppies. You didn't try to escape." She then gave me an extra pat and said, "You even tried to warn me! Thank you!"

My chest swelled with pride. Sophie glanced over at me, and her look told me that she was also proud of me. That made me feel so good. In a way, I wished I had been braver to go exploring with the others; but at the same time, following the rules felt good too.

Once we had been herded back into our puppy area, Mom gave us a stern reprimand. She told us that we needed to behave, or we could get hurt. Running away to the unknown was not allowed. We all nodded that we understood, but looking at Murphy and Danny whispering to each other, I doubted this was the last escape adventure we would see. Mom went over and stretched out on top of the platform to discourage any more escape attempts. Once we realized that we were trapped, we suddenly all felt tired from our adventures. We all grabbed our favorite snuggling toy, found comfy nap spots, and we all quickly fell asleep for a nap. We all slept so soundly that we didn't hear Cam making changes. We certainly were surprised when we discovered that the low walls around our puppy area had been replaced by a wire fence while we slept. The fence made our area much larger, and Cam had added some more beds and new toys to the area as well. Danny, of course, hopped up onto the table but was dismayed to discover that the fence in this new area towered over him by several feet.

Later that afternoon, Cam opened the gate on our new pen and led us outside and onto her deck. As soon as my paws landed on the deck, my nose was bombarded with all sorts of new smells. There were earthy smells, musky smells, floral and woodsy smells, and even the fresh scent of far-off rain. I was overwhelmed and had to sit down to think about all these new scents. I also watched as my siblings ran to explore this new space.

Sulley spotted a puppy-sized ramp and ran up the ramp at full speed. I think he was expecting another table or platform once he reached the top, but he quickly discovered that the ramp immediately sloped down after reaching its high point at the edge of the plastic swimming pool. Sulley was running so fast that he ended up in the middle of the pool before he stopped! This was perfectly fine with Sulley, and he continued to run and jump into and out of the pool. The pool wasn't quite deep enough for him to swim, but he was having a wonderful time running up and down the ramps.

After a while, Sulley realized that, if he took his running start from the deck, he could jump all the way into the middle of the pool without using any of the ramps. Sulley barked at Cam, who came and added some water to the pool, making it deeper for his jumps. Cam took a short video of Sulley jumping and commented that she would send it to Sherry. I had fun watching him play in the water, but I really didn't want to get wet myself.

Molly noticed a ramp next to the deck stairs and scurried down into the yard. She got to the grass and suddenly stopped. I could see the look of confusion on her face. The grass was cool and sort of like the carpet inside, but it was up to Molly's elbows. It tickled her tummy. She stood there for a few minutes, sniffing the grass and pawing the ground before deciding that there was nothing to worry about. A few minutes later, I did see a worried look across her face; but this time, her worried look was that there were no treat stations in the yard. Molly flopped down on the grass with a very frustrated sigh. When Cam happened to look in her direction, Molly became overly dramatic about the lack of treats. Her drama did not change the outcome.

Cam continued to enrich our experiences and give us more things to learn. Some days, she had her people friends visit. We learned quite a bit about each person as we sniffed them. Sometimes we could tell that a person had a pet at home just by smelling them. Now and then, some of Cam's friends would bring their own belly puppies with them. That's what dogs call human babies. They aren't dog puppies, but as people puppies, they are learning about their world, just like us.

We loved when the belly puppies—children—came to visit. They usually giggled a lot when we licked their faces, and they tried to chase after us. Their moms and dads tried to teach them not to pull on our ears and our tails while Cam and Morgan tried to teach us not to nip or chew on them. I bet it was just as hard for the kids to learn as it was for us to learn our lessons too.

We spent a lot of time in the yard, which was really exciting to me. I loved all of the different smells and enjoyed sitting in a patch of sunshine, just sniffing the air and watching all the activity around me. Cam came over to me one afternoon and commented on my air of calm amidst the chaos of the other puppies. She gave me the nickname Zen puppy.

That was the same day that Murphy was trying desperately to get to something under Cam's shed. He was absolutely certain that there was something under there, and he needed to get to it. Cam did not allow him to dig, but he still tried to crawl under the building. He displayed that "terrier tenacity" and was absolutely unwilling to give up his hunt.

Cam noticed that Whiskey was playing on the new agility equipment. His fearless nature led him up the tall, tall ramp and across the bridge and down the other side. Morgan barked her encouragement and then led Whiskey through the weave poles and then over a series of jumps. Whiskey ran back to try the course on his own and was quite impressive as he ran and jumped and hopped through the obstacles. He ran through the tunnel without hesitation and was even unafraid as he rode the huge teeter-totter as it thumped down.

Sophie, meanwhile, was playing with Cam's friend Roy. Roy was showing Sophie the basics of how to behave in a dog-show ring, including the proper trot and how to stand for the judge to admire her. Roy was so patient, and Sophie wanted to show how well she could listen. From where I sat, I admired Sophie and marveled at how Roy could make her look even more beautiful.

Danny ran from place to place, joining everyone in their games. He didn't seem to be able to stay in one spot for very long at all. He noticed me sitting by the fence and came over to make sure that I was okay. I assured him that I was enjoying the sunshine, the breezes, and watching everything. He playfully nudged me and challenged me to a race to the water bowl. I happily chased after him, and we laughed together as we got our drinks.

Molly went from point to point looking for treats. I watched her paw Cam's leg gently, but each time, Cam explained that there were no treat stations outside. Molly finally gave up, huffed her displeasure, and went over to a shady spot under a tree and sat down. I hoped that Molly's forever home would have lots of treat stations, but I also doubted that there would ever be enough treat stations to make Molly completely happy.

I looked around and realized that Whiskey was trying to climb up on the table. His sensitive nose had detected some sandwiches, and he was determined to get to them. I don't think he was as interested in the food as he was in the challenge of getting to them. He was trying to drag one of Sulley's ramps toward the table when Cam realized what he was up to and moved the sandwiches into the house. Whiskey sat down next to me with a disappointed look on his face but then brightened and commented that he'd figured out an easier way to move the ramp. He could always find something good in anything.

Each day, we all got a little bigger and stronger. Our puppy teeth came in, and we all loved chewing on things. We had some tough rubber toys that felt really good to chew on, especially when Cam cooled them in the refrigerator. Murphy got in trouble one day for chewing on Cam's shoes, but she admitted that she should not have left them where he could get to them.

Our days were filled with fun activities. We played chase and steal-the-toy and ran all over the agility equipment. Sulley spent most of his outdoor time in the pool, and Cam even let Whiskey try his paw at pulling a small cart. It was demanding work keeping Whiskey busy enough to keep him out of trouble. I sort of felt sorry for Whiskey's future family because they were going to have to work really hard to keep that guy busy.

It wasn't all fun and games, though. Morgan was teaching us our puppy manners, and she nipped us if we got out of line. Morgan made sure that we learned proper body language and how to interpret what other dogs were saying to us. When you stop and think about it, we were all learning two languages. We were learning how to communicate with people, but at the same time, we had to know how to talk to other dogs. The interesting thing is that some of our "words" in dog are completely misunderstood by people. For example, people thought that Murphy was smiling when he showed a wide, toothy grin. In dog language, he was trying to tell everyone that he was unsure and asking everyone now to give him some space. I don't blame the people for not understanding. I've been a dog my whole life, and I sometimes get things wrong.

Meanwhile, Cam tried to teach us not to jump up on people, but we all disobeyed that lesson—we were always so excited to see other people, not because we didn't love Cam, but because we wanted to get more rubs and scratches from the other people. There were other lessons in people language that she taught us. "Sit" and "come" were easy. The "stay" command was really, really hard. None of us liked having to wait in one place until we were called.

Cam taught us other important things. She would tell us to go to our rooms, and we would all run into our crates. She fed us some of our meals in our crates. Our favorite toys were in there, and most nights, we slept in our crates. I felt safe and secure in there and would sometimes go into my room when I just wanted some alone time. Once or twice, Sophie joined me in my room, and we occasionally snuggled in there for naps.

Morgan made sure that we learned to potty outside. Sometimes it was hard to wait, but we all tried extra hard. Cam was good about taking us outside after we ate, played hard, or woke up. We learned to ring bells to let everyone know that we needed to go outside. Cam was always thinking of things to help us settle into our new homes as smoothly as possible.

Every couple of weeks, Cam would put us into the crates that she kept in her car, and we would all go see the doctor. Puppy doctors are known as veterinarians, and they have special tools and medicines for puppies. Most of our visits were quick. The doctor's assistants would weigh us, take our temperatures, and make sure that we were all healthy. I did not mind those visits. I even didn't mind when Dr. Armen would come in and give us shots! They pinched a little, but he explained to us that the shots would keep us from getting sick. He always gave us extra rubs and treats for being so brave.

After the excitement of the trip to the doctor, Cam would take us home and put us back into our exercise pen for our naps. We did not take as many naps anymore, but it was still comforting to snuggle with everybody. Occasionally Murphy would have a crazy dream, and he would move his paws like he was running in his sleep. I made the mistake once of sleeping near his feet. Never again! I was kicked several times. Now I knew to sleep next to his back. Cam took a lot of photographs when we were all snuggled together in our "puppy pile." We had settled into a nice routine of eating, playing, napping, and playing. Life was incredibly good, but every so often, either Cam or Morgan would mention our new forever homes. We were all a bit anxious about this upcoming change, but Morgan told us everything would be fine. She encouraged us to make the most of our time together. We tried to, but it was still a little worrying.

One night, I saw Cam moving our crates around a bit. She set a box on top of each crate and then a bag into the box. I wondered if that meant that we had another visit with Dr. Armen coming up although we always used Cam's crates on our other trips to see him. I sort of hoped we weren't going to see the doctor again. I liked Dr. Armen well enough, but I did not really want any more shots! I decided to wander over to get a closer look at what Cam was doing. It was unusual that she was organizing things into the bags, so I really wasn't sure what was going on.

As I sat and watched, I saw Cam putting all sorts of things into those bags. I saw a book with a picture of a wheaten terrier on it go into each bag, followed by a comb, a brush, and a toothbrush! Next came a stack of papers, a bag of treats, and a leash. She also included in the bags our new toys just like our favorite toys, a small bag of treats or two, and a water bowl and a couple of bottles of water. Cam even included a couple of baggies of dog food. It was easy to tell which bag was Molly June's because Cam had put an extra packet of treats into that bag.

I was surprised to see Cam hang each bag from a hook on a grooming table. Cam had put each of us onto her grooming table every few days and brushed our hair, tickled our toes, and brushed our teeth. She wanted to make sure that we were all comfortable with that routine, and I learned later that one of her last jobs for us would be to teach our new parents some basic grooming steps. While she didn't include scissors in the bag, she did have pictures and information on the various kinds of scissors and places that sold them. I think Cam thought of everything!

Leaning against the table was a folded exercise pen. I didn't know it then, but that was going to be helpful for the ride home. I also saw that there was a comfy-looking pad inside of each crate. I started to look forward to this new adventure, wherever it might lead.

Most of our crates had the table behind it with the bag on the hook and the pen next to it, so I guessed that Cam was setting up these things for each of us. But I still couldn't figure out why. Molly came over to see what was happening when Cam rustled a bag of treats, and Molly looked disappointed as the treats went right into the bag.

By now, we were all watching Cam, and we talked among ourselves to try to figure out just what was going on. Morgan came over to where we were all sitting, and she barked softly to get our attention. We all sat quietly around our mom to hear what she wanted to say.

"Cam has picked out your new homes, and over the next few days, each one of you will be going to your forever homes. She has spent a lot of time talking to your new people, and she has matched you to new families who will love you, play with you, and let each of you grow up to be happy and healthy dogs."

She went on to explain that Cam was sending us home with everything that our new people would need to keep us happy, healthy, and properly groomed.

It was incredibly quiet as that message sank in. Then everyone chimed in all at once with questions.

"Where will we be living?"

"When do we meet them?"

"Will I like them?"

"What is it going to be like?"

"Will there be other puppies?"

"What about belly puppies?"

"Any cats?"

Sulley asked about a pool. Murphy asked if there would be stuff to hunt. Molly June wanted to know how many treat stations her house would have. Whiskey asked if there would be agility games and sandwiches. I didn't ask many questions. Sophie and I sat quietly, feeling glum. We knew that we would miss our brothers and sisters and were just a little worried about what would happen next.

Morgan came over to where we were sitting together. She looked down at us and gave us each a gentle hug. "You two are my thinkers. You will be fine. I know that Cam has picked out perfect families for you. I know that change is hard sometimes, but this is for the best."

Sophie looked up at her with her beautiful brown eyes brimming with tears. "But we will miss you!"

I nodded my head in agreement. Morgan assured us that we would forever be in her heart and she would hear about us from Cam when our new people shared their stories about us.

"I hope that we hear about you too," I murmured.

Morgan gave me a hug and assured us that she would make sure that Cam told our new people about what would be going on with her as well.

Sophie and I looked at each other, then at Morgan. I swallowed hard, trying not to cry. I didn't want to upset Morgan or Sophie, and I was trying to be brave.

I leaned over to Sophie and said, "We will have fun meeting our new people and having all sorts of new experiences." I only wished I felt as brave as my words.

Sophie leaned against me and whispered, "Thank you for being the best brother, Quincy."

I licked her ear and whispered, "And you're the best sister ever."

We stretched out and fell asleep snuggled together. Together we dreamed about our new homes and what adventures were ahead.

A New Home, a New Family

A few days later, the door opened early in the morning, and some new people came into the house. Cam welcomed Laura and Conrad and told them that she had Sophie's things ready to go. They came to where we were all playing, and Danny broke away from our game. He was, of course, first in line to say hi, with his tail wagging happily. He was our litter's ambassador, fearlessly greeting everyone who came to the house. The rest of our group trotted over behind him to get pets and belly rubs from Conrad and Laura and to give kisses in return. We all pushed and shoved each other to get the most attention we could from these wonderful new people. Laura and Conrad were careful to make sure that they greeted each of us; and we all got belly rubs, ear rubs, and lots of kisses.

Cam invited Laura and Conrad into the puppy room, and we all followed. Laura sat down on the floor as soon as she came in. We swarmed all over her, climbing into her lap and giving her kisses, as all our tails wagged as hard as they possibly could. Meeting new people is always exciting! After a little while, Cam reached down and gently picked up Sophie from the wiggling puppy pile. She handed her to Laura, and Laura gave Sophie a tender hug.

Sophie looked over at us with a bit of concern in her eyes at first. Why had she been singled out from the group? Laura kissed Sophie, and Conrad reached down and petted Sophie a bit. Laura held Sophie close and whispered something in her ear. Sophie looked at Laura, and I saw her tail give just a bit of a wag. Cam handed Laura Sophie's favorite purple elephant toy, and Sophie snuggled down into Laura's arms with her toy. Sophie looked down to the rest of us looking up at her and yipped softly to let us know that everything was going to be okay. She wagged her tail a little bit more and yipped again to let us all know that she liked her new people. With a contented sigh, she settled into Laura's arms. We then understood that Cam had picked Conrad and Laura to be Sophie's forever parents, and Sophie agreed with that decision.

After talking with Cam for a few more minutes, while Laura continued to snuggle Sophie, Conrad took Sophie's crate, exercise pen, grooming table, and her bag and carried everything out to their car. Once he was back inside, Cam had Laura put Sophie on the grooming table and showed Laura and Conrad the routine of brushing, toe tickling, and teeth brushing that she had been following with each of us. Laura said that she was glad to learn Sophie's ticklish spots and that she looked forward to getting her ready for dog shows. Sophie looked like she was enjoying the attention and behaved perfectly for Laura.

Once done with the grooming lesson, Conrad and Laura talked a bit more with Cam, and then he and Laura carefully passed Sophie back and forth while they took turns giving Cam a hug. With that, they went out to their car, put Sophie in her crate, gave her a few kisses, waved goodbye, and drove away. They had a long drive back home to California and wanted to get started on their trip.

After the door closed and things were quiet again, we looked around at each other. It dawned on us that Sophie was on her way to her forever home with Laura and Conrad and she wouldn't be playing with us at Cam's house any longer. A cloud of sadness came over all of us, and we sat quietly and looked at each other.

Morgan came over, and she quietly barked, "The first to leave is always hardest on the ones left behind."

I understood completely what she meant, and I secretly hoped that no one else would be leaving for a long, long time. Goodbyes are hard. My wish of no more goodbyes wasn't going to come true, though, because I watched more of my brothers and sisters leave to join their new human families over the next few hours.

Sulley was next to leave. We didn't know that the new people who had come into the house were going to be Sulley's new parents as we greeted them. They were excited to see our wiggling pool of puppies, and again we enjoyed kisses and belly rubs. Danny was especially interested in Mike's shoes and tugged on the shoelaces. Mike noticed this and bent down to tie his shoe again, fluffing Danny's hair as he told him that his shoes needed to stay tied so that he didn't trip and fall.

We wondered who would be going home with these nice people when Cam picked up Sulley and put him into Sherry's arms. We watched as Mike and Sherry hugged him, and I heard Mike tell Sulley that they had a swimming pool at their house in Florida that was just waiting for him. Sulley was excited about that and was anxious to get there and try it out. Mike laughed and told him that he had a long car ride first.

Cam gave a brief grooming lesson and pointed out that Sulley's hair should be rinsed after he went swimming to keep it from getting tangled. We watched Sulley carry his toy dolphin with him as he settled in his crate for the ride.

Cam gave Sherry an extra paper. "Here are some excellent dog life jackets that will come in sizes small enough to fit Sulley. As much as Sulley likes the water, you will probably want one for his trips on your boat."

Sherry agreed, noting that Sulley would need a smaller jacket than the one she had from her first wheaten, Bailey. Sulley's tail wagged even harder at the prospect of having a boat. While this discussion was going on, Mike held up Sulley and looked at him carefully. He then turned to Sherry and Cam and said that "Sailor Sulley" would carry on the traditions started by "Bosun Bailey" perfectly. Another goodbye wave, and we were five puppies, all feeling a bit sad.

Morgan called us all together to have lunch. I think we were all hungry, but coming together and having our lunch from the big bowl in our play area highlighted that two of us were missing. After eating, I went over to one of our beds and stretched out to take a nap. I figured, if I went to sleep, I couldn't think about Sophie and Sulley.

The excitement of the morning had made me very tired, and it did not take long at all for me to fall asleep. As I slept, I had a dream about Sophie and Sulley! I dreamt about Sophie going from dog show to dog show as everyone admired her beauty and Sulley riding in his boat with the wind flapping his ears and the salt spray making him sneeze. When I woke up and thought about my dream, I hoped that they were going to have as much fun in real life as they were having in my dreams!

A little later that afternoon, there was another knock at the door. Murphy's new person, Patricia, had arrived. Cam set up an exercise pen in the front yard and carried Murphy out and set him into the pen. We all watched with interest from the front porch—this was different from our other goodbyes. With that, we saw Patricia bring another wheaten from her truck, and the new dog and Murphy touched noses through the fence of the exercise pen. Patricia brought Murphy's new big sister, Reilly, with her to meet Murphy. This introduction was done out in the front yard since it was a place that was not familiar to either Murphy or Reilly.

After the nose touches and tail wags were done through the fence, Patricia lifted Reilly into the exercise pen with Murphy. We again watched as they introduced themselves with lots of sniffs, tail wags, and a few play bows. Cam and Patricia took Reilly and Murphy from the exercise pen and then put the rest of us into the pen. Once again, we had the first introductions through the fence of the exercise pen as Reilly and Murphy touched noses with us.

Cam and Patricia lifted everyone into the pen with Reilly and Murphy, and we all listened closely as Riley told us stories about flying all of the way from Canada to come to live with Patricia. Murphy was excited to talk to Reilly about rats and mazes, and the two of them were deep in conversation by the time they were in their crates, and Patricia started to drive toward home in Connecticut. Cam gave Patricia two stuffed toy rats for the pups to play with during their ride home. I will admit that I felt just a little jealous that Murphy was going to have another wheaten to play with at his new home.

Speaking of flying, Whiskey got to fly to his new home in Florida! Whiskey was worried and wondered if there would be anyone to play with on the airplane. His bag of toys and treats went into a box to travel along with Whiskey. Whiskey would travel safely tucked in his crate, and Cam put Whiskey's toy llama in the crate to keep him company during his trip to his new home with Jeanne.

Cam's friend Jay had come to help her, and together they carefully lifted Whiskey's crate and box into his truck. Fortunately, Jeanne already had a grooming table and exercise pen, so those things did not need to be shipped along with Whiskey.

Cam had asked Jay to drive Whiskey to the airport and get him all settled for her flight. He and Cam had sent puppies this way before, so they knew all of the forms and papers that had to be attached to Whiskey's crate. I hoped that Whiskey would be comfortable and safe in his crate and wished that we could meet Jeanne to put our lick of approval on his new parent. This felt very strange, saying goodbye without any hellos to go along with them.

Once Jay had driven away, Molly June, Danny, Morgan, and I looked around. The room felt very empty with the others gone. Morgan tried to reassure us, but I was really sad. Danny, ever the optimist, tried to convince us that everything was going to be just fine and that our families were on their way to get us; but I could see that he was worried and just a little bit scared too.

Morgan explained that Cam had set up a schedule so that our new families did not all arrive at the same time. This gave her the time for a bit of a chat with each family and to give them her grooming demonstration. The new parents would also have time to ask questions and to get to know their pup a bit before they left and were on their own. That all made sense, but it was hard to wait. I wanted to meet my new people! As excited as I was about that, I also didn't want to have to leave Cam and Morgan.

Cam came over, gave us all hugs, and told us that we were going to have one more sleep at her house and we'd be going to our new homes the next day. Danny, trying to be helpful, suggested that we play some games to fill the time. I wasn't sure I wanted to play, but Danny always made everything so much fun that I couldn't resist joining in.

Later that evening, Cam made an exception and did not close our crates when we went to bed. She was barely out of the room when I quietly woofed to Molly June. She woofed back, and we met in the big bed in the center of our play area. We had just gotten comfortable snuggled together when Danny came and threw himself into the bed. We laughed as we shifted to make room for him. It felt wonderful to be snuggled in one final puppy pile with Molly June and Danny. I didn't fall asleep immediately but instead listened to everyone's quiet snores. I was going to miss them, just like I already missed Whiskey, Murphy, Sulley, and Sophie.

Everything felt wrong the next morning. After breakfast, when we all went to our play area, it was just too quiet. With only the three of us puppies in the space, it felt huge and empty. All of the toys were there, but we could really feel the absence of the others. Even Morgan seemed a little sad as she stayed with us in our play area instead of going to sit with Cam.

We were not in our play area that long when Molly June's new family arrived to take her home to Delaware. As usual, Danny was the first at the door to greet Denise and Jim but moved out of the way when Denise scooped up Molly and told her of all of the exciting treat stations waiting for her. I thought that Molly was going to burst for all of her excitement.

Still holding the squirming Molly, Denise bent down and gave Danny a special ear rub. "We used to have a special boy who looked just like you. His name was Charles. I miss him terribly, but I know that you're a special boy and that you will be happy with your new family."

I could see a look of sadness cross Denise's face, but she brightened when Molly June reached up and gave her a bunch of kisses. Molly seemed to always know how to make someone feel better. Jim put Molly June's bag, exercise pen, and crate into their car and then took Molly from Denise's arms. He held her extra close and murmured that it felt so good to have a wheaten in their family again. He gently set Molly June into her crate with her stuffed iBone toy that looked just like Cam's iPhone and told her that she could call her friends on the ride home. Molly June wagged her tail and gave the toy a few squeaks to let him know that she understood.

After they left, Danny and I talked about what adventures we thought might be ahead for each of us, trying to ignore the fact that we were going to soon be separated. I understood even more clearly what Morgan had meant the day before about goodbyes being hardest on the ones being left behind. I was already missing my sisters and brothers.

It wasn't very long before the door opened again, and Danny ran to the door where he met Di and Rob from Michigan. He tripped over his own feet as he ran into Rob's ankles and skidded to a stop with a plop! Everyone was laughing as Rob picked him up and handed him over to Di. Di told Danny that they had come to take him home to his new house. Danny wagged his tail so hard that I wondered if it would fall off! His new people seemed really nice, and Di offered each of us homemade cookies that she had brought. She also gave Cam a bag of treats for Morgan and a container of something for herself.

Cam admitted that she had been hoping that Di would bring one of her gourmet specialties with her, and Di didn't disappoint. I thoroughly enjoyed the cookie and felt a little sad for Molly, who missed out on this wonderful treat. Then when I thought about it a bit more, I was actually sort of glad that Molly June wasn't there to see what treats she would be missing so she didn't feel badly. I was even happier when Di gave me an extra cookie! These homemade goodies were delicious. Danny was pretty lucky to be going to a home where someone could make such delicious treats. As before, Cam gave a brief grooming demonstration to Di and Rob; and with that, I was the only puppy left at Cam's house.

Once the others had left, I quietly sat next to Morgan. I was feeling sorry for myself. I was missing all of my brothers and sisters, and I was starting to worry that there wasn't a special family for me. Morgan tried to reassure me that my family was coming for me and that this was all according to Cam's schedule, but I wasn't really listening. I was so deep in my own sad thoughts that I didn't hear the car pull up, and I jumped when the door opened again. Were these my people? They were! Mom and Dad had come for me from New Jersey, and I think they were as excited to meet me as I was to meet them.

Dad came over next to where Morgan was sitting and bent down to pet her. She was happy to have some attention from him and leaned against his legs while he rubbed her ears. Then he reached over and picked me up. It was a long way from the ground to his arms! He held me gently, and I felt completely safe and secure in his big and strong hands. Curiosity got the better of me, and I started to wriggle and twist a bit. I don't think I was ever that far from the ground, and I wanted to look all around!

Cam and Mom talked a little bit about the distance from my new home to Molly June's new home. My ears perked up a bit—maybe Molly and I will be able to see each other again! I sure hoped that we would.

Cam pointed out the things that she had assembled for me to take with me, so Dad reluctantly handed me over to Mom. She held me on her shoulder so that I could watch what was going on; and she and Cam chatted while Dad carried my crate, grooming table, pen, and bag out to the car. Once Dad came back in from loading the car, Mom put me on Cam's grooming table, and they learned how to take care of my hair and nails. Cam also remembered to tell Mom that my feet are very ticklish and that I would prefer that they not be touched.

After the grooming session and while the people stood talking, I was nestled in Mom's arms. I was so excited and relieved to have my own people that I couldn't stop giving kisses. After a few minutes, though, I suddenly realized, though, that Morgan was going to be alone with just Cam when we left. I started to cry a bit. Everyone thought I needed to go to the bathroom, so we walked to the yard. Morgan came along with the group. When they put me on the grass, I made sure to go potty, but then I ran over to Morgan to give her extra kisses. Morgan gave me a few kisses, then nudged me to go back over to Mom. She quietly explained that she was happy with Cam and that she was looking forward to having Cam all to herself. She told me that she had other puppies go to new homes before, and while she would miss us all, she was incredibly happy that Cam had picked such good homes for each of us.

We walked back inside, and Cam made sure to hand my favorite toy to Mom. Mom then put Kitty next to me in her arms, and we all walked out to the car. Dad gently took me from Mom and put both

Kitty and me into my crate. I was glad to have Kitty to snuggle and settled into my crate for a nap while we traveled.

As we drove away, I looked back and saw Cam hugging Morgan. They both looked happy but tinged with just a little bit of sad. I knew just how they felt. We were all starting a new adventure, but we would miss all the fun that we had together.

The ride to my new home seemed to take forever! The movement of the car was very soothing, though, and I curled up in my crate to take a nap. I was happy I had my stuffed kitty to snuggle with, and even though Mom was sitting next to my crate, I still felt very lonely. I accustomed to napping to the sound of lots of contented puppy snores.

After we had been traveling for a while, Dad stopped the car. He got out and set up my pen. Mom scooped me out of my crate and set me down on the grass in the pen. Morgan and Cam had taught us all what to do, so when Mom told me to go potty, I was happy to obey. I was enjoying all of the new smells when Mom picked me up and set me back into my crate. She left the door open while I had a drink of water and a treat, and then she closed the door. While I was having my snack, Dad folded the pen and put it back into the car. A few minutes later, we were on the road again.

The car started to move again, and Mom leaned against my crate as we traveled. This time, I wasn't as sleepy, so I tried to look around a bit more. Mom saw me sitting up, and she reached into the crate. I was happy to crawl over to her fingers and gave her a bunch of kisses. She reached down somewhere with her other hand and then poked a treat into my crate. Yum! This treat was cheese flavored—my favorite! Unfortunately for Mom and Dad, I was getting tired of being in the crate and started to cry. I was really feeling pretty sorry for myself. I missed my brothers and sisters. I wanted to run and play. I missed my mom. I missed Cam. I wanted to go home.

Mom carefully turned the crate so that the door was pointing toward her and opened the door. She reached in and put her hand gently on my back.

"I know it's scary, Quincy," she said. "I know you're missing your brothers and sisters, but I promise you we will love you more than you can imagine."

I was reassured by her words. Her hand felt really good against my back, but I couldn't let her know that right away. I continued to cry, but my whimpers became softer and softer as I drifted off to sleep again. As I napped, I had a dream of my siblings all together again playing in a field filled with other wheatens. It was a beautiful dream, and everyone looked so happy.

I don't know how long I napped, but I woke up when the car stopped again. Mom was moving her hand away and reaching for my leash. I assumed we were stopping for another potty stop. Mom lifted me out of the crate and put me on the seat next to her. She got out of the car, scooped me up again, and set me down on the grass. Dad had not set up the pen this time.

It was also much quieter. The earlier stop was filled with cars and trucks and people all coming and going. This was a quiet street, much like Cam's house. There were no other people moving about, and I only heard one car drive down the street while I was standing there.

Mom said, "We're home!"

I looked around for a minute, hoping to see Cam and Morgan, but I realized that Mom meant we were at their home. It wasn't my home yet. While Mom walked me around a little while I stayed close on my leash, Dad moved all of the things that they had gotten from Cam into the house.

Mom and I started toward the stairs. Mom paused to see if I could climb them on my own. I didn't want to try and look like a fool if I couldn't, so I simply sat down and looked up at her. She gently picked me up from the sidewalk and set me down on the front porch. Dad had left the house door open, so after Mom opened the storm door, we went inside.

"Welcome to your new home, Quincy," Dad said to me.

I looked around more than a little uncertain. I didn't see anything that looked familiar. I didn't even see my crate anywhere! I plopped down on the floor and whimpered a little. Mom came walking up to me from another room and put Kitty down next to me. At last! Something familiar and comforting.

I was still wearing my leash, so Mom gently guided me through the house. I intuitively knew which room was the kitchen! There were some good smells coming from there. I saw my big comfy bed in the room Mom called the TV room, and I felt just a little better seeing that in this new house. The bed was too big for me, but it was my bed. It had the smells of all my brothers and sisters and Morgan on it.

Mom and I walked down the hall, and I then saw my crate in the bedroom. Mom had put something of mine in every room so that I would feel more at home. I suddenly realized that she really would be taking loving care of me.

We went back to the TV room. On the way by, I had a quick drink of water, which made Dad decide that it was time for me to go outside for another potty break. We went through another room and two doors onto the deck. This was a completely new place for me to investigate!

Dad took my leash off and carried me down the three steps to the backyard. I paused and looked up at Dad. Surely he didn't mean to remove my leash. I couldn't see any sort of fence or barrier. I could run away!

Well, in theory, I could. We know that Danny would have wandered off somewhere. Murphy might have considered it if he heard something, and Molly June would likely have gone looking for treats. But I didn't want to go too far away from Mom and Dad. I sensed that would make them sad, and they were so nice to me that I didn't want to upset them. I did wander around a bit where I could still see them and discovered that the grass was tall and it tickled my tummy!

I "did my business," as Dad put it; and then with Mom's encouragement, I started to wander around the yard a bit, keeping them in sight. I smelled rabbits, and chipmunks, and maybe even a mole. I didn't smell any other dogs, though.

After a few minutes, I realized that I was getting tired. This was a huge area, and it was going to take me a few days to explore the entire place. I looked around and saw Mom and Dad sitting up on the deck, so I started running toward them. Dad saw me running in their direction, so he called my name and said come. I got to the foot of the stairs, and Dad reached down and lifted me up onto the deck. He also gave me a cheesy treat!

Dad said, "Good 'come,' Quincy," as he gave me the treat.

We went back into the house, and we all walked to the TV room. Mom lifted me up onto the couch and put me onto a blanket folded next to her. She rested her hand on me, and that felt really good. I settled in for another nap. I decided that this was going to be a good place to live, and I was looking forward to whatever new adventures I might have. I was happy Cam picked this mom and dad to be my new mom and dad.

School Days

While we were living with Cam and Morgan, we learned the most of basic puppy lessons. A lot of the lessons from Morgan helped us learn how to talk to other dogs. Most of the lessons were to help us know how to behave if we met another dog. There are so many ways that we pups communicate! Of course, we bark and growl, but we use our whole bodies to communicate as well.

Almost everyone understands the easy messages. A growl or ears pulled back means "I don't like this. Please stop!" A wagging tail means "I'm happy!" Rolling over for a belly rub says several things, including "I trust you." Some messages are a little harder for people to decipher, but dogs know right away what they mean. For example, when I bow down with my tail high in the air, I'm inviting you to play. We call this a play bow.

Barks are not easy for people to understand either. Barks could mean "Go away. You're not welcome," or "Hey! You're here. I'm saying hi!" Some dogs bark because they're bored, just like some people talk to themselves. Morgan worked hard to teach us because, if we didn't understand something a bigger dog said, either by body language or bark, we could get hurt.

Cam and Morgan worked together to teach us that it was okay to be in our crates. Cam made sure that we each had comfy beds in our crates, and she often fed us in our crates. She wanted to make sure that we thought of our crates as good places. I learned to like my crate so well that I would sometimes nap in my crate when I didn't have to. Morgan showed us how much she liked her crate, and we learned from her example.

They also taught us the basics of potty behaviors. We learned to go to the bathroom after we woke up or played or ate. We did not always make it to the designated spot on time, but we tried. Neither Morgan nor Cam got upset with us if we had an accident. They understood that we were just babies, and we just weren't ready yet.

Cam sent us home with a packet full of information that included training notes. Our new parents could read about what commands we had learned and what words Cam used, as well as some online places they could go for more details. Cam stressed that it was extremely important that our new parents commit to continuing our education to help make us canine good citizens. Once we got to our new homes, our new people continued to reinforce these first lessons. I was so proud of myself when I went an entire day without a potty accident! That didn't happen every day, but I tried. I also practiced sleeping by myself all night in my crate. I didn't mind, but I think I would have liked to have been up on the big bed with Mom and Dad. But I couldn't jump up there on my own. I guessed that I would have to wait to sleep up there until I was more grown up.

One afternoon, Mom gave me an extra brushing. I was a bit confused about that since she normally brushed me in the evenings while they watched the television. I had been happily chewing on my green snake squeaky toy when she scooped me up and deposited me on the grooming table. I wasn't particularly interested and tried to squirm off of the table, but she firmly told me no and stay! I could tell she was serious by the tone of her voice! I didn't realize people could growl too.

Anyway, once I settled down and resigned myself to standing up and getting brushed, it really wasn't too bad. I especially liked the one-on-one time with Mom as she carefully and gently teased out any knots in my hair. She stepped back after a while and told me what a handsome pup I was, and she gave me another piece of cheese. I wasn't surprised about her telling me of my handsomeness, but I was surprised by the bits of cheese. I paused to wonder if the grooming table was a treat station at my sister Molly June's house. Molly expected treats everywhere!

Mom also used a little buzzing machine to smooth my toenails. That tickled! She told me that she didn't want to cut my toenails too short, so this was a safer tool for her to use. I remembered that Cam had clipped a nail too short once, and I was happy to learn that Mom wanted to avoid that. I will admit that my toes felt good with the shorter toenails.

After she had brushed my hair completely, she took me into the people bathroom. She lifted me into the bathtub and turned on the water. I scrambled to get out of the way of the water, but it didn't work.

"Silly boy, you have to stay in the bathtub in order to get your bath!" She laughed.

Mom held tight to me, and I was soon soaked to the skin. I think we were both surprised how small I looked when my fluffy hair compressed to my body.

Dad walked in and jokingly asked, "Where is the rest of Quincy?"

I looked to be about half the dog I was before my bath.

Mom then took some of the shampoo that Cam had sent home with me and gently lathered it into my hair and skin. It smelled really nice, and I liked the massaging of her fingertips. Maybe this bath thing wasn't so bad after all. She was extra careful around my face, and she didn't get any suds into my eyes. I was very happy about that. After the shampooing, Mom rinsed the soap from my hair and then carefully rubbed in another good-smelling liquid. This was a conditioner and was intended to make it easier to get knots out of my hair. After letting that soak in for a minute or so, Mom carefully rinsed every bit of conditioner from my hair. She even rinsed between my toes, and I will admit that tickled a lot.

When she was done, she lifted me out of the bathtub and onto some fluffy towels. She tried to wrap me in one of the towels, but I was faster and gave myself a really good shake. Water droplets flew everywhere. A few more shakes and a bit of a rub with the towel and I wasn't very wet any longer.

Imagine my surprise then when Mom lifted me back onto the grooming table! This time, she used a different brush and a pair of scissors and carefully cut my hair. She didn't cut a lot of hair off, but she did make me look a lot neater. She was especially careful with my beard, barely taking anything off. She told me that she was letting it grow long on purpose. While she was clipping, Mom commented to Dad that she was glad that Cam had included grooming instructions in my welcome bag. She acknowledged that I wasn't getting ready for a dog show but instead just getting neater, and the instructions really helped.

Mom also left some of my hair longer on my forehead and let it fall down between my eyes. She explained to me that this was a traditional look for wheaten terriers. She told me that a lot of people complained about not being able to see a pup's eyes and that they didn't understand that the hair over a wheaten's eyes would protect their eyes if they were hunting. I wondered if Murphy had a fall of hair between his eyes. I also wondered if Mom wanted me to start hunting. I really hoped she wouldn't ask me to.

Once my haircut was complete, Mom lifted me down to the floor. I really wanted to run outside and rub my face along the ground, but Mom wasn't letting me go outside. I settled for rubbing my face along the couch and running around like a crazy pup.

Mom and Dad both laughed and said to each other, "Bath-time zoomies!"

I finally wore myself out and flopped onto my bed in the TV room for a nap.

After Mom and Dad had dinner that night, they put my harness onto me, and we walked out to the car. I tried to jump in my myself, but I wasn't quite big enough to make it all of the way up onto the seat. Mom reached down, picked me up, put me on the seat, and then put my seat belt onto me. It wasn't like the ones that they wore, but instead it clipped into my harness. I didn't really like it because I could not reach them to give them kisses. But I could look out of the window and move around a little bit, so I guess it wasn't all bad. Dad told me I had to wear it to keep me safe if he had to stop the car quickly.

I could tell by the sounds that we were heading toward my doctor's office. I was a bit puzzled because I wasn't feeling ill, and

I remembered Dr. Barbara saying that I had gotten the last of my puppy shots when I saw her a week or two ago. When we passed her office and we didn't turn into her parking lot, I realized that we were going somewhere different.

We rode for a while, then we stopped at this nice-looking farm. The smells were different. I wanted to sit and enjoy them, but Mom encouraged me to walk with her into the building. As we walked in, I could see that there were other puppies on leashes sitting with their people all around the room, and we all looked at each other with curiosity.

Mom, Dad, and I went over to the side and sat down. Mom got up and took some papers to a friendly-looking person, and he put them into a folder. I heard him thank Mom for my vaccination records. I guess he needed them to make sure that we were all protected from getting sick or making someone else sick.

After a little while, the friendly guy came and stood before the entire group. He told us that his name was Joe and that he was going to be our teacher. He also introduced us to one of his dogs, Tucker, who would show some of the things he wanted us to learn. Tucker really was the teacher's pet!

Before class started, Joe invited one of our parents to bring each of us to the center of the room so that we puppies could all meet each other. We used all of our senses to learn about one another. Obviously we looked at each other. We sniffed each other. We listened to each other. We barked at each other, and a few even licked another dog. I learned that I was the only wheaten terrier in the room and that my classmates included a pit bull named Jada, a briard named Bonnie, a miniature schnauzer named Madison, a Bedlington terrier named O'Toole, and a Labrador retriever named Moose. We were allowed to play together for a little while, and then Joe told our people to take their seats.

The first night, we learned some simple things that I already knew, thanks to Cam, Mom, and Dad. He had Mom and Dad tell me to sit and then give me a reward of a little piece of cheese. I thought that the next command was a funny command to have to learn: "collar." When they said "collar," they were to grab my collar.

Joe explained that this was a good command for everyone to know so that I wouldn't be startled if someone grabbed my collar. I didn't mind. I got a piece of cheese every time they reached for my collar. We also learned "look." For that command, I was supposed to look at Mom's or Dad's eyes. That was a little hard for me to do since Morgan had said that looking someone in the eyes was a challenge and could lead to a fight. I guess that rule only applies to dogs. The lesson lasted about an hour. By then, I was pretty tired and fell asleep on the ride home. I wondered if there would be more lessons.

I soon learned that there would be more classes. Over the next few weeks, our lessons got increasingly involved. I felt really good because I had learned some of the commands before I officially started school. By the end of the third week, I knew "sit," "look," "collar," "down," and "off." I think it was more confusing for the people in the class to remember the difference between "down," which meant we were to lie down with our chests on the floor, and "off," which meant we were to stop jumping. "Off" was extremely hard for me to remember. I simply believe that everyone deserves a proper wheaten greeting consisting of much bouncing and licking. Joe did not agree for some reason. I suspect that was because Tucker did not know how to do a proper wheaten greeting.

As we had more or less mastered the first set of commands, Joe had us move onto more difficult commands. We learned "heel," which meant to walk next to Mom or Dad without pulling or falling behind. Coupled with that, I was to sit next to Mom or Dad's leg when we stopped walking. As with the easier commands, when I did things the right way, I was rewarded with a bit of cheese. If I forgot what to do, everyone was patient, and I got to try it again until I got it right.

Another difficult command for me was "stay." I didn't like having to sit and wait for them to call me because I wanted to be with them all of the time. We started out with short wait times, like five seconds, and gradually extended the time I had to stay where they told me to and wait for them to call. It took a lot of practice both at school and at home until I could stay where I was supposed to most of the time. The best part about "stay" was the matching command, "come." I could barely contain my excitement when they called me to come to them. I had to remember to run behind them and then sit next to their left leg in order to get the cheese reward.

Joe also stressed two other commands and explained that they were for my safety. "Stop" meant I was to stop and drop to the down position without hesitation. I was also supposed to stay in that spot until Mom or Dad called me. Joe explained this command needed to be learned so that I never hesitated and so that they knew I would always stop when told to. "Leave it" was another command for my protection. When "leave it" was told, I was to drop whatever was in my mouth at once. As long as it wasn't cheese, I was okay with the command. Sometimes Dad tested me by telling me to leave it when I had a piece of cheese. It was so hard to obey under those circumstances. I finally got to where I could do it every time. I didn't like it, but I did it.

One evening, my entire class went outside to one of Joe's fenced-in areas. I recognized the agility toys that Cam had had at her house. I wasn't really excited about agility games, but I was proud to show off that I knew what to do with the different pieces of equipment. Joe had another of his pups, Scout, run through the course to show. I was amazed—she was so fast! She ran the course with a confidence that came from years of practice.

Joe had to adjust the equipment heights between students, so he made sure that we always went in order, from Madison to Bonnie— from shortest to tallest. Even as a puppy, Bonnie towered over me. I wondered how big she was going to be when she was fully grown. That was a fun evening and a bit different from the drills we had been doing in the training room. I could see, though, how those other lessons applied to agility because we had to really listen to our people and follow their direction. I guess it all came down to trusting each other and paying attention to each other.

Right before I graduated from puppy school, we had a special test. Just like people have standardized tests, dogs do too. Joe had someone else come to our school to make sure that the test was managed properly and that the test was the same for everyone. You have no idea how hard it was for me to sit with Mom and Dad and not go running over to give the new person a proper wheaten greeting! I wanted to impress the new person, though, so I stayed next to Dad. I did wag my tail a lot, though.

The special test was to see if we would earn the important title of Canine Good Citizen. This test evaluates ten skills that prove that we have good manners. A couple of the skills were a little hard for me because I had to suppress my wheaten excitement. Accepting that a stranger wanted to talk to Mom was okay, but when I had to sit politely to get pet, I had to keep reminding myself to sit. I wanted to bounce up and give them kisses.

I was perfectly content to let the testing person brush me and play with my feet. That was something I'd been accustomed to since I lived with Cam and Morgan. When the test lady bent down to pick up one of my feet, I gave them a little lick on their arm. She laughed a little and made a note in her book. I was afraid that I had really messed things up, but she told us to continue to the next part of the test.

Mom and I took a short walk, and I were careful to stay right next to her. Since I might have made a mistake by sneaking that lick, I didn't want any more bad marks. Mom and I continued to walk when we came to a little group of people. They moved a little bit, and we walked right on through the middle. Mom told me we could come back later and I could give them a wheaten greeting then if I just kept walking with her this time. That sounded like a fair deal.

The next hardest part of the test for me was the "stay." Well, really it was a combination task. First I had to sit, then go down and rest my chest on the floor, and then Mom said "stay" while she walked to the other end of the room. I was so excited when she called me to come that I almost forgot to go around behind her and then sit at her left side. Just at the last minute, I remembered, and that made me feel good.

Joe had a surprise for us during the test. He had another of his dogs with him, so when we were assessed to see how we would react to a strange dog, she really was a dog we didn't know. Mom and Joe walked toward each other, paused to chat, and then walked on. I would have liked to meet and greet his girl Serena, but that would have to wait until after the test was finished.

When Joe and Serena left the room, the door banged quite loudly. I was startled by the noise, but it didn't really bother me. I did turn to look at the testing lady when she dropped her notebook. A few papers flew out, and I watched them flutter about but knew that I couldn't pick them up for her.

The last test was hard. Mom told me to sit and then asked the test lady to "watch Quincy." Mom then left the area! I looked around a little but then thought about it. She always came back when she left, and this lady seemed nice. I'd just sit there and wait a few minutes and see what happened. And Mom came back! I stood up and wagged my tail, then remembered that I was taking a test, so I sat back down. The testing lady gave Mom my leash and said that I was a very good dog!

The next week was our graduation ceremony from Joe's class. The first thing he did that evening was to give out the certificates to everyone who passed the Canine Good Citizen test. We also got yellow bandanas and a tag to wear on our collars. Then Joe had his own final exam for his class. His test was a lot of more fun than that Good Citizen test because we could win prizes for following our commands. I was the best at "come" that night, running faster than any of my classmates, so I won a long squeaky snake and a bag of peanut butter treats. I honestly think those were better prizes than the bandana.

After my last class, we took a different way home. We stopped at a place with a funny name, Tootie's Ice Cream, and Mom ordered a "pup cup" for me. I wondered if that meant that there would be a puppy in a cup but quickly realized that it meant a small dish of delicious ice cream for me. Mom chose the vanilla and peanut butter flavor, and I was happy to lie in the grass lapping up that delicious treat. I was a little disappointed when I finished it, but to tell the truth, my tongue was a little tired and very cold. I hoped that we would come back here again. I liked my pup cup.

After I had lived with Mom and Dad for a while, I noticed that it was getting colder when we went outside. I didn't mind the cooler weather. I preferred it to the heat of the summer. Autumn brought new smells, including wood smoke and crisp leaves.

One morning, I was having fun chasing after some of the falling leaves when Mom called me to come in. I didn't really want to but thought that she might have some cheese for me. When I got inside, I was surprised when she gently put something onto my back. She adjusted a few straps and clips to make sure that it was comfortable for me. There was a handle in the middle of my new backpack that she used to confirm that the straps were snug enough to keep the pack from moving around when I walked yet loose enough that it did not pinch. She unbuckled my pack, and I watched as she put a couple of bottles and a flat disk into one of the pockets. She also put a baggie of treats into my pack. Yum! Snacks on the go!

I then noticed that she was holding two other packs. Those other packs were much larger, and I was both confused and concerned. I didn't think that there were more dogs in our pack, and even if Mom and Dad had gotten more dogs, I didn't think that they would get big dogs. I stood there looking at all of the packs when Mom noticed my confusion and explained that she and Dad had their own packs. Now why would they be wearing packs? I wondered.

Dad snapped my leash to my harness while Mom gathered all three packs, and we went out to the car. They buckled my harness into the seat belt, and we drove off. Dad put the windows down, and I enjoyed the breezes flopping my ears and sniffing all of the wonderful smells. After a while, Dad parked the car and grabbed the packs from the back of the car. They put their packs on while I waited, and then Mom put my pack onto me and again made sure that the pack was adjusted properly. While she was doing that, I looked around to see where we were, but I didn't recognize anything. I could smell some things that were familiar, but there were other plant and animal smells that I did not know at all.

Mom took my leash, and I hopped out of the car. Dad followed behind as we started to walk on a dirt trail. This was something new and different—I had never experienced a dirt trail before. A few times, we had to pause while Dad lifted me over a tree that had fallen across the trail, and there was one spot where I had to walk across some water that was flowing over the trail. That water made me realize that I was thirsty; and it must have had the same effect on Mom and Dad because, a little farther down the trail, we stopped for a drink. I was surprised when Mom took the disk out of my pack and pressed on it a bit and it became a bowl. She took one of the bottles from my pack and filled the bowl. That water tasted so good! She also gave me a couple of my treats while they ate their protein bars and had some of their own water.

Mom and Dad talked a little and decided that we had gone far enough for my first hike. We turned around and retraced our steps back to the car. I had a little more confidence on the return trip and even tried climbing over one of the trees by myself. I certainly was tired by the time we got back to the car!

That was my first hike, but it certainly was not my last. We hiked the local parks very often, but I even got to hike a bit of the Appalachian Trail, some trails along the Skyline Drive, and even in the Great Smoky Mountains. Whenever I would see my pack come out, I would get very excited. I loved those times.

I really loved weekends. Mom and Dad were home from work, so anything was possible. Many weekends, we went for hikes and then came home and worked in the yard. While they worked in the yard, I would go sit by the fence and watch what was happening in the neighborhood. I could see almost everything, and I enjoyed just watching everything. I rarely barked since I was usually just observing the routine activities of everyday life.

I also enjoyed taking naps on the porch swing that was in the backyard by the firepit. Dad never put a fire in the pit during the day, but I liked sitting on the swing with its gentle rocking motion. That chair had a nice cushion, so it was extra comfy as well.

As I got bigger, Mom and Dad let me do more and more fun things. I was really excited the first time that they invited me to snuggle with them up on the big bed. In fact, that first time, Dad had to lift me up. It was so high up in the air. And it was so wonderful. There were pillows and blankets, and it was warm and snuggly. I loved sleeping up there. I felt so loved and happy.

To be honest, I think Dad wanted me to curl up down by their feet to sleep, but I was so excited to be there with them that I wanted to sleep up closer to their hands. I slowly crawled up inch by inch and made myself comfortable between them. I sighed contentedly when Mom put her arm over me, and I felt her love flow all over me. I was a little concerned that Dad would realize I was there and make me move, but that fear went away when he reached over and rubbed my ears a little. I knew then that I wasn't going to have to move to the foot of the bed. We all went to sleep snuggled together. It reminded me of the puppy pile that I shared with my sisters and brothers at Cam's house so very long ago.

I know that some people have little things that they do to help them relax or to make them comfortable when they're a little worried. Sometimes it's something like counting things, like the number of steps from one place to another, or it might be to hold on to a favorite toy or blanket. Dogs have things that give themselves comfort too. For me, I liked to lick things, especially blankets or hands. Even though I was extremely happy on the big bed, I liked to lick the comforter to help me relax and get sleepy. Mom used to tease me a little bit about it, but I think she found the sound of my licks comforting too. Dad wasn't too happy, though, when he would accidently put his hand into the damp spot!

We settled nicely into a comfortable life. I spent my days taking naps in sun puddles in the living room, surveying my backyard by walking the perimeter of the fence, greeting visitors, and cuddling with Mom and Dad. We would take road trips to hike in distant places, and I learned how to behave when we stayed at hotels or other people's houses. Occasionally, when we would visit other places, there would be other dogs for me to play with. Those times reminded me of how much fun I had with my brothers and sisters, and I felt just a little bit sad. Mom and Dad would tell me stories that they read about them, but I missed cuddling with them.

In spite of that, I was happy living with Mom and Dad and loved them very much. Cam and Morgan had picked the perfect family for me.

A Trip to the Mountains

One autumn day, when I was about a year old, I was napping on the big bed. The windows were open, and there was a wonderful breeze with interesting smells. I was startled awake when Mom started to put neat stacks of clothing onto the bed. I rolled over to see what she was doing and watched as she laid out jeans, sweaters, shirts, and other bits of clothing. She then gathered some other items from the bathroom and added them to the growing collection of things on the bed. I inched a bit closer to see if I could gather any sort of clue to tell me what was happening.

Dad came in and sat next to me. He was thoughtfully rubbing my ears when he said, "And the plan still is that I'll come down in two weeks. You sure I can bring Quincy?"

My ears certainly perked up when I heard my name, so I listened very closely to hear what Mom was about to say.

"Yes, and the motel is dog friendly. Just bring his crate so that we can safely leave him in the room if we need to."

That certainly sounded interesting, so I sat up to make sure that I could pay attention.

Mom saw me sit up and reached over to scratch my chin. "Don't worry, Quincy. Dad will take good care of you while I'm away." Mom started to transfer the things from the bed into a duffel bag and commented, "And if I forget anything, you can always bring it along."

She looked up and realized that Dad had left the room and that she was just talking to me.

She chuckled slightly and said, "I'll remind him, Quincy. You don't need to worry about telling him."

With that, she zipped the bag closed and carried it out to the living room. She opened her briefcase and looked inside, then closed it. She commented that she had several notepads and her laptop, so she should be all set for the class.

I had followed her out to the living room and was surprised to learn from her comment that she was going to go to a class. I hadn't realized that people went to classes too. I wondered what sorts of things she would have to learn. She carried her bags out to the car and then double-checked to make sure that she had her cell phone, wallet, and keys. I stood at the door and watched her and wondered if she was going to leave without saying goodbye. She always paused when she left for work to give me a hug and a kiss on my nose. I would have been extremely disappointed if she changed her routine while leaving for this trip.

Mom came back into the house and gave Dad a hug and a kiss. I tried to squeeze between them, but they kept moving so I wasn't successful. Finally, Mom bent down and gave me a hug and a kiss. The hug was a bit longer than usual, so I had time to give her ear a lick. She whispered in my ear that I should listen to Dad and be a good boy and she'd see me in two weeks. I wasn't entirely sure how many sleeps equaled two weeks, but I was sure that it was more than two or three. I wasn't very happy that she was leaving for that long, but no one asked me about it.

With that, Mom went out to the car, got in, and drove away. I sat at the door and watched until I couldn't see her car anymore, then turned and looked at Dad. I felt sad and empty. Mom and Dad both left every day to go to work, but this was different. I looked up at Dad, and he reached down and fluffed the hair on the top of my head.

"Yes, we'll both miss Mom while she's away. But we can also look forward to visiting her in Virginia."

I didn't know what Virginia was, but the way Dad said it, it sounded pretty interesting.

Dad and I fell into a new routine. He went to work during the day while I napped. That was the same as before Mom left. In the evenings, though, instead of getting to smell the wonderful smells as Mom fixed dinner, Dad would bring home a bag of food for his dinner. He would sometimes share his french fries with me or a tiny piece of his cheeseburger, but there were no tasty bits of home-cooked dinner in my bowl. Dad tried to make it up to me by putting extra cheese on my dinner, but it really wasn't the same thing.

One evening, I saw Dad putting a few of his things into a duffel bag. I wondered if we were going to see Mom! I watched as he measured out scoops of my food into baggies and then put the baggies into another bag, along with a couple of my bowls. It certainly looked as though he was getting ready for us to go to see Virginia and Mom. Imagine my disappointment then when he crawled into bed as usual and we hadn't gone anywhere at all.

Ever hopeful, I thought that we might leave in the morning, but his morning routine hadn't changed. He got up, got himself ready for work, gave me my morning treats, and left for work. I looked longingly at the bags on the dining room table, wondering why he had gotten everything ready, but we weren't going anywhere.

After a long day, one that felt even longer and more lonely than usual, Dad finally came home from work. He surprised me by not bringing home his dinner bag but instead went straight to work, taking my crate apart and putting it into the car. He put the bags he'd prepared the night before into the crate and clipped my travel harness onto me. I started to get really excited! He snapped my leash onto the harness, and we walked out to the car. I happily hopped up into my place in the back and waited for him to attach the tether to my harness. The tether kept me from moving around too much in the car and would keep me safe if he had to stop very quickly.

Dad then got into the driver's seat, and we were off! We only went a little distance when Dad stopped the car. I didn't like where he stopped—the smell of gasoline was very strong, and it made my nose twitch. We weren't there long fortunately, and he then parked the car close to the building.

"I'll be right back, Quincy. Guard the car!"

I didn't know how much guarding I could do from the back seat, but I did sit up straight and watch the people coming and going. No one came close enough to our car that I felt that I needed to bark at them, but I did bark a bit of a greeting when I saw Dad coming back.

He had a bag of food with him, and I was happy to see that he'd gotten a little bowl with some food for me. I took my time and savored the delicious mix of cheese and hamburger while Dad ate his cheeseburger. He ate more quickly than I did, so I was still eating my dinner as he pulled out of the parking space. We were on our way!

The movement of the car was gentle, and I started to feel quite sleepy. I curled up into a ball on the seat and took a nice long nap. I was vaguely aware of the music that Dad was listening to, but it really didn't make that much of an impression on me.

When I woke up, I was surprised to see that it was dark outside. We were also surrounded by lots of big trucks, and I could tell that we were going fast. I started to feel a little scared, so I whimpered and cried a bit. Dad tried to reassure me, but he was busy concentrating on the road and keeping us safe. I guess I was feeling a whole mix of emotions—scared, confused, and sad—and while I tried to stop crying, it was very difficult. I know that I was making Dad feel bad, but I really couldn't help it. After a while, I fell back to sleep, so all was quiet in the car again.

I wasn't asleep that long this time when I felt Dad pull off of the highway and then drive a little while until we pulled into a parking lot. He left me in the car while he took our bags somewhere, then came back empty-handed. I wasn't worried about the bags, though, because I saw Mom walking behind him! I was so excited to hear her. I cried again, but this time, they were happy cries.

Mom snapped my leash onto my harness and unclipped the tether and led me over to a small patch of grass. I could smell the other dogs had been there before, but I didn't know any of them. I quickly pottied and turned to see Dad carry my crate into the building. Mom and I walked behind him, and we went into Mom's room.

As we walked in, I noted that it looked like a little house. There was a kitchen, a bedroom, and a bathroom. The kitchen had a few good smells, so I could tell that Mom had been fixing tasty things to eat there. The bed looked quite inviting. It wasn't as high as the one at home, so it was quite easy for me to jump up onto it.

While Mom and Dad sat and talked, I stretched out on the bed. It felt so much better now that we were all together again.

We all got up early the next morning, and Mom got ready and then took me outside for my morning potty trip while Dad was getting ready. We then all got into the car and buckled our seat belts and safety tether, and we were off on an adventure. We drove on a highway for a while, then turned off onto narrow and twisty roads. I could feel that we were going up, and that was a strange sensation. I'd never gone up a hill quite so large before. Mom and Dad were talking about the possibility of going over to the Valley, but they didn't want to make the day too long.

As we continued up the big, big hill, I sat watching the trees go by. There was a low wall along the road, and I could see beyond to even bigger hills.

Mom reached back and gave me a quick ear rub and then said to Dad, "I wonder what Quincy's thinking. I don't think he's ever seen mountains before."

It was just about that time that Mom pulled over and parked the car. She said that she wanted to take a couple of photos from the scenic overlook. We all got out of the car, and we walked over to the rock wall. While they were taking pictures, I was sniffing all of the exotic smells. I could tell that there were lots of different animals in the area, and the air was so clear and fresh. I took several deep breaths, really enjoying the mountain air. Once they were done taking their pictures, we all got back into the car, and we continued driving up even farther.

At the second scenic overlook, I already knew the routine. I hopped out of the car—with my leash securely clipped to my harness, of course—and put my paws onto the rock wall. I looked around, sniffed the good smells, and then looked up at Mom and Dad. I could tell that they were really happy and relaxed. They had obviously been to these mountains before, and they brought back good memories for them.

The third overlook was a little different. There was a huge flat rock that was at the same height as the rock wall. Mom encouraged me to walk out onto that rock a little bit so that she could take a few pictures of me. I trusted her that it was safe and she wouldn't ask me to do anything dangerous, but I really didn't like being up that high. I was quite relieved when she called me, and I could cautiously walk toward her and then hop down next to them.

We drove on a little farther, then drove out of the mountains and into a small town. Mom seemed to know where she was because she drove us straight to a little building. They opened the windows a little bit and told me to be good. They were going to get something to eat and promised to bring something to me.

I don't know if it was all of the excitement of the mountains or the drive the prior evening, but I was happy to have some quiet time to take a nap. There was a nice cool breeze coming into the car, and I had a lovely sun puddle to curl up in for my nap.

It didn't seem very long at all when Mom and Dad came back, and just as they had promised, they had lunch for me. It was a delicious cheeseburger. Dad had carried a bag with french fries out of the restaurant with him, so they sat and munched on their fries while I enjoyed my meal. After I finished, Mom gave me a bowl with water, and then we walked over to a far corner of the parking lot so that I could potty.

Once everything was cleaned up, we resumed our journey. I assumed that we were in the Valley because I could see the mountains on either side of the car. The trees were turning beautiful golds and yellows and reds, and the mountains looked as though they were covered with a rich carpet full of autumn colors. I could see why Mom and Dad liked this area so much.

The movement of the car lulled me again into a peaceful nap, and I could hear the murmurs of Mom and Dad's conversation in the front seat. I thought about what a lucky pup I was as I drifted off to sleep.

When I woke up, we were again on the highway, and it was getting dark outside. I heard Mom ask Dad if he wanted to get something for dinner before they got back to the motel or go to one of the places she had found during her stay. The decided to go on to the hotel so that I could relax in the room while they ate.

It didn't seem to be that long before we arrived at the motel, and while Mom took me for a short walk to the potty place, Dad carried the small bag with my bowls and treats into the room. Even though I'd had some good naps during the day, I was glad to see my crate. I always felt safe and secure in my room, and I knew that I could relax while Mom and Dad had their dinner. They left the TV on so that I had some noise to keep me company, and I stretched out and relaxed until they came back.

Just as I'd hoped, they brought some of their leftovers with them, and Dad mixed it in with the kibble he had brought from home. I enjoyed the little bits of chicken as a treat. I didn't get chicken very often. I had a mild allergy to it, and if I ate much of it, I'd get really bad earaches. I could have a taste of it once in a while, and that made it even more of a treat.

The next day was fairly quiet. Mom and Dad got up and went to the motel restaurant for breakfast and brought back a small bowl of scrambled eggs for me. I enjoyed my breakfast while Dad packed up his things and carried my crate and his bag out to the car. I was a little sad when I realized that we were leaving without Mom and sat really close to her while she and Dad talked.

Dad stood up, signaling that he was ready to leave, and Mom bent down to give me an extra-special hug and nose kiss. She thanked me for coming to visit her while she was in class and said that she would see me again in about a week. She and Dad hugged, and then we all walked out to the car. Dad clipped my harness into the car, and we were on the road again.

The drive home was uneventful; and while I was glad to get home again—back to the familiar sights, sounds, and smells of my backyard—I still missed Mom. I hoped that the week would pass quickly.

Dad and I settled back into our routine without Mom. Dad would get up and go to work, and I would nap on the couch. Each evening, when Dad got home from work, I would look past him, hoping that Mom would be coming into the house behind him.

With each passing day, I became sadder and sadder. Dad noticed this and gave me some extra treats, and we would sit together on the couch.

"I miss Mom too, Quincy."

Dad reassured me that she would be home soon, but I was starting to lose hope.

Friday started out exactly the same as the other days that week. This time, though, Dad didn't bring his dinner home with him as he had been while Mom was away. I wondered about that and was pondering this change in routine when the front door opened and Mom came in! I was so happy to see her that I zoomed around the living room, jumping from the couch to the chair to the floor and back again. Round and round I went, stopping every third or fourth circuit to jump on Mom and let her know just how happy I was to see her.

After a few more circles, I settled down and sat in front of Mom. She reached down and gave me a big hug and a kiss on my nose. She whispered into my ear that she had missed me and then turned to Dad and asked about dinner. Dad laughed and suggested getting a pizza. Mom groaned a bit and said that she had been looking forward to a home-cooked meal. Dad had already gone to call in the pizza order, so I followed Mom to the TV room and sat next to her for extra cuddles.

Later in the evening, I reflected on the events of the day. Mom was home, and she and Dad had pizza, leaving the crusts of the pizza to share with me. We called the crust pieces pizza bones, and they were one of my favorite people foods. We were all together again, and the day ended with cuddles and pizza bones. What more could I have wished for?

Quincy's First Christmas

The first time it happened so gradually that I didn't notice at first, but there was a distinct chill in the air. I don't remember exactly when I noticed that the air was getting even cold enough that Mom and Dad started putting on extra clothes to go outside. I was relaxing on my favorite outdoor chair and got frustrated when Mom and Dad kept making me move from my resting and observation spot. It seemed as though I would just get comfortable, and they would make me move. They would take the cushion away. Grr. I watched as they gathered everything from the yard and put it into the sheds. They said that they were getting ready for Winter. I wondered who Winter was and what Winter had against comfy cushions.

One morning, a few weeks later, Dad opened the door for me to go outside; and I started to run across the deck at full speed. Suddenly my feet wanted to go in four different directions. I slowed down and got my feet under me and looked back to see Dad laughing at me. He was trying not to, but he was having a hard time hiding his laughter. I stood up and walked more carefully out into the yard. The ground was covered with fluffy white stuff. It looked like the stuff inside of some of my stuffed toys, but it was cold. I tried to bite some, but it disappeared in my mouth. It tasted a bit like a shredded ice cube, but I knew that couldn't be what it was—there was just too much of it. Besides, when would Mom have had time to shred that much ice?

When we went back inside, Mom asked me what I thought of my first snow. I wagged my tail to let her know that I thought it was a lot of fun and that I'd like to play with it again. She laughed and said that I'd had enough for today but there would be other snow days coming up.

One night, a few weeks later, Dad left for work really, really early in the morning. It was still dark outside! He said something about snow, and he had to go in to work early because of it. But when I went outside to potty, there wasn't any snow on the ground. Mom and I went back to sleep for a while after Dad went to work. After we got up, I was surprised to see Mom put her coat on when she said it was time for me to go outside. She normally stood at the door to watch me, so she usually didn't need her coat.

She opened the door, and I stood there looking out over an unfamiliar landscape. There was a thick blanket of snow over everything! I couldn't tell where the steps were or where the path was. Everything was covered. Mom used a shovel to clear a path for me to get to the steps, but I couldn't wait any longer. I ran off of the steps and suddenly found myself in fluffy, cold snow up to my armpits! I struggled to move forward but quickly figured out that, if I hopped from spot to spot, I could move about the yard relatively easily.

While Mom cleared off more of the deck and the steps, I played in the snow. I jumped over the same area a couple of times and created my own path through the snow. I ran, rubbing my face in the snow until I got snow up my nose, and it made me sneeze. I rolled around in it, waving my legs in the air. It certainly wasn't dignified behavior, but it was fun! Mom was laughing as she recorded some video of me playing. She said that she would have to show it to Dad later.

I was sort of glad when Mom called me to come inside. I was a little cold and very tired. A nap was going to feel particularly good. When I got into the sunroom, though, I realized that Mom wasn't going to let me go straight to my nap. I had little snowballs stuck to my hair all over my body. She took some pictures of my snowballs and said that it looked like I had been attacked by several bags of marshmallows that were stuck all over. I licked a few, but they just tasted like snow.

Mom took me back to the bathroom and put me in the bathtub. She ran warm water over me to melt the snowballs, and it felt really good. I was a little afraid that she was going to give me a bath, but instead she wrapped me in some fluffy towels and rubbed me really well to get most of the water off. That didn't stop me from shaking a few times and flinging water everywhere. Finally, I was dry enough that I could go take my nap. As I drifted off to sleep, I thought about how much fun I had in the snow.

We continued to have snow periodically, every few days in fact. Sometimes it was enough snow that Dad had to go to work; other times, it was just enough for me to play.

One evening, I saw Mom drag a huge red bag in from the garage. I could not begin to imagine what might be in that bag, so I curled up on the sofa to watch what was going on. Meanwhile, Dad was bringing in several boxes, also from the garage. Once he'd brought in the boxes, he flopped onto the futon next to me, and together we watched Mom pull tree branches from a box and string some sort of green rope onto those branches.

Both Dad and I took a brief nap while Mom continued building her tree, and I was startled when I opened my eyes to see a huge pine tree before me in the living room covered with millions of colored lights. I hopped down from the sofa and wandered over to this new tree. I gave it a careful sniff, and Mom and Dad both called my name. I turned to look at them.

Mom said, "That's a Christmas tree. You are not allowed to touch it. You may not leave *presents* under it."

I chuckled to myself. I knew not to go to the bathroom in the house, and I realized that Mom and Dad thought that I might be confused about the indoor tree.

I moved over to the side and watched as Mom and Dad took turns hanging things onto the tree. Every now and then, they'd hold one up and talk about where, or when, or why they got that particular ornament. Mom held up a little angel holding a tiny wrench.

She showed it to Dad and said, "Remember this one? I got it for you the year you transferred to work in Moorestown."

Dad grinned and said that he remembered. He then held up a tiny ornament of a curled-up cat. "Jerry gave this to you, am I right?"

Mom agreed, and they started to reminisce about Jerry and that family. I realized that Mom and Dad had lots of memories about places and people, and these ornaments were reminding them of good times. I felt a little sad that I didn't have any memories to share while decorating the tree. I guessed that just wasn't a thing for dogs to do.

Later that evening, Mom came over to where I was sitting. She was holding a beautiful coat in her hand, and I was surprised when she put the coat over my back and reached under my tummy to attach a few straps.

She stepped back and said to me, "Quincy, you are the most handsome wheaten terrier in world."

My chest swelled with pride, and Dad called me so that he could see me in this wonderful coat. As I passed the mirror in the hall, I paused for a moment and decided I agreed with Mom. The beautiful wine color of my coat was especially nice.

When Dad and I walked back into the living room, I saw that Mom had removed the now-empty red bag along with the boxes. She had put a pretty cloth on the ground under the tree, and she was admiring her work. I walked over and sat down in front of the tree, and with that, Mom stepped back a little. Dad called my name. I turned to look at him, and Dad snapped a photograph. Mom then asked that I lie down in front of the tree. I did as she asked, and they were soon agreeing that one of those pictures was perfect.

Mom left Dad and I in the living room, and I heard some thumps and clanks. We listened intently for several minutes, and then Mom came into the living room with a jar that she uses when she takes her lunch to work. She also had a bag of cheese cubes. Were we about to have a party?

Dad clipped my leash onto my coat, and we started out of the house. I was surprised to go out the front door; and it was then when I realized it was dark, snowing, and very cold. Dad had me hop up into the back of the car, and they settled into the front seat.

For the next hour or so, Mom drove us around the neighborhoods, and we looked at the lights hung on houses and trees. There were a few homes where it looked as though they had put a light onto every single blade of grass. Others had a spotlight shining onto something that they wanted to highlight.

I will admit to taking a short nap but was more than happy to wake up when Mom offered several cheese cubes. I nibbled on those while we looked at a few more homes and their displays of lights and other decorations. Some homes even had music.

I sat back and thought about it a little. People seemed to pick certain days to highlight with special activities. I remembered people decorating for Halloween and then people coming to the house dressed very strangely and calling out, "Trick or treat!" Then there was Thanksgiving, where Mom and Dad went to her sister's house and met with a lot of their family. Of those two holidays, I liked Thanksgiving best because Mom shared some of the turkey with me. Yum! Now we were celebrating Christmas with an indoor tree and a trip to look at outdoor lights. People are funny sometimes.

A few weeks later, Mom took out a turkey that had been thawing in the refrigerator and did some of her "cooking stuff" and put the turkey in its huge pot onto the stove. It didn't seem to take long until the delicious fragrance of roasting turkey filled the air. I certainly hoped that Mom would share some of the turkey with me again this time.

Much later that afternoon, Mom disappeared into the kitchen again. I could hear pots clanking and the sound of Mom chopping something with one of her knives. Curiosity got the better of me, and I went and sat at the door into the kitchen. Dad spotted me there and called me to join him in the family room. I reluctantly got up and followed him as he went into the TV room and hopped up onto the couch. Dad explained that he was trying to keep me safe.

I think both Dad and I had dozed off because the doorbell's ring made us both jump a bit. Dad went down the hall and greeted Mark and Catherine as they came into the house. I tried to remember my lessons, but I ended up jumping on them a bit. It's almost impossible to not give everyone a wheaten greetin' full of bounces and kisses.

The doorbell rang several more times, and each time, I tried to behave as more people came into our living room. It was so exciting to see all of our friends at once, and everyone was talking and laughing. I hadn't noticed when a second table was added, but it certainly was necessary as everyone took their seats. I sat back a little way and looked at the assembled group. There were Mark and Cat, of course;

but also at the table were Katie, Dee, Stephan, Pam, Barbara, Parviz, Toni, and Jan.

The kitchen counter was filled with all kinds of food, including the carved turkey, some ham, and lots of potatoes, both sweet and regular. There were vegetables, rolls, a small cheese plate, gravy, and more things that I couldn't identify. Everything smelled so good. There were special dishes throughout on the counter and the table, all pointing the mind back to a childhood home or a special place filled with memories. The makers of those special dishes told the story of the treat and why it was special.

And I scored! During dinner, I walked about under the tables, resting my head on people's legs to see what food I might be lucky enough to get. I soon figured out that Pam was an easy touch. I could count on getting something from her each time I tried. At the same time, Dee was impossible. She wasn't going to share anything with me! I stole Stephan's napkin right from his lap. I had a wonderful time! Eventually I went over to the sofa and decided to stretch out on the floor in front of it. I wasn't sure I could jump up; so full was my tummy. I listened as the clanking of forks slowed at the table, and the conversation and laughter remained strong.

Mom left the table at some point, and helped by Mark and Jan, they packaged the leftover food and put it in the refrigerator. The dishes were either washed and put away or carefully stacked off to the side. Mark wiped the counter off; and then more plates appeared on the counter—cookies, pies, and candies. The special treats continued to appear, including Iranian cookies, chocolate babka, Danish pancakes, and a huge plate of cannoli. Mom set out a plate with homemade caramels, butter mints, and hard candies. Dad put Stephan in charge of making coffee while Jan helped with the tea. Soon everyone had a steaming mug in front of them, and everyone settled back around the table.

Mark excused himself from the group for a few minutes and went outside to his car. When he came back inside, he was carrying a magnificent cake in the shape of a Christmas tree, complete with presents all around it. Everyone laughed as they realized that there were several tiny presents for everyone, complete with tiny bows and name tags. Mark said that he had made the tiny gifts so that everyone could take some cake home to enjoy later.

Toni wordlessly pointed to several packages that had my name on them and looked at Mark. He laughed and explained that they had just peanut butter or yogurt for icing and that he had taken a few of his dog's biscuits to "wrap." He didn't want to leave me out of the festivities.

Toni took one of my little presents from beneath the cake tree and gave it to me. I carefully carried it over to my bed by the tree and chewed on it thoughtfully. Having friends to share the holidays with made them even more special. As I lay by the couch on my comfy bed, I could feel the love in the laughter and felt so cozy and warm. I decided that Christmas was my most favorite holiday of all.

More Adventures

It was a frigid day in February that I watched as Mom got out their big duffel bag and started to pack it with sweaters and jeans. Dad came into the room and asked if he should grab their snowshoes.

Mom paused for a minute or two and then said, "Why not? There's plenty of room in the car."

Dad left to get them while I sat wondering what made a snowshoe a snowshoe. I had seen them with their regular hiking boots and dress-up shoes. They had tall boots that they wore in the snow and other shoes that they would wear depending on their planned activities. What made snowshoes special?

Dad came back into the room and said that the snowshoes, poles, and boots were in the car. He added that he had found boots for me and that they were in the car as well. My ears perked up on that sentence. I didn't even know that I had boots! I was now extremely curious to learn more about my boots, but I could tell that I would have to wait until another time.

A bit later, with the duffel bags, my crate, and a small bag with my food and bowl, we were on our way. I didn't know where we were going, but I was excited just to be going along with Mom and Dad.

I really liked riding in the car. The gentle motion of the car, coupled with the gentle hum of the tires on the road and the soft conversation from Mom and Dad, usually lulled me into a nap; and this time was no different. I'm not certain how long I napped, but when I woke up, the landscape had changed significantly. Instead of the grassy roadside that I was watching before my nap, I saw instead craggy rocks rising high above the car. I looked anxiously at Dad to see if he was worried that the rocks might fall onto us. But he seemed totally unconcerned, so I decided I didn't need to worry.

We traveled for several hours through an ever-changing landscape. After the craggy mountains, we drove along a highway that was bounded by tall trees on both sides. We finally pulled off of the highway and into a small town. It looked a bit like home, but I could tell that it wasn't.

A few more turns and we stopped in front of a neat house. Mom and Dad got out of the car and stretched and then clipped my leash onto my harness, and I hopped out. Mom took me to a patch of grass near the street for me to do my business, and I was happy to have a chance to potty. Mom cleaned everything up, and we walked up the sidewalk to the house.

I paused to sniff the funny-looking goose on the porch. It was dressed in a raincoat and even had a rain hat. One sniff and I realized that it was actually a decoration and it wasn't a real goose.

Just then, the front door burst open, and we were all swallowed up in a hug.

Dad exclaimed, "Zelda!"

There was much excited talking at once. Zelda—whom I later learned was really named Diane, just like Mom—turned and told her husband, Walt, to give Dad a hand with our luggage. I got really excited when I realized that we were going to be visiting Zelda for a while.

As we went into the house, I caught a whiff of another animal, but I didn't see anyone else. No one came running to greet us. I guessed that something must have been near an animal and picked up its smell. I promptly forgot about it.

Well, that was a mistake. The next morning, after breakfast, I was exploring a little bit. As I walked into the kitchen, I smelled that animal smell again; and this time, it was much stronger. I wandered over toward the kitchen table and suddenly realized that there was a cat curled up on one of the chairs. How had I not noticed her before?

I inched closer to sniff her a bit more when she fluffed her fur and suddenly looked three times larger. She also hissed and extended her paw with a quick swipe toward my nose. I backed up quickly. She missed my nose, but I certainly didn't expect that. I took a couple of steps forward again, and the cat stood up. Uh-oh, I didn't want to risk those claws coming toward me again, so I backed up and went to the other side of the kitchen.

I hadn't realized it at the time, but Mom and Zelda both watched my encounter with Abigail Snotty Cat. Apparently Abigail didn't like much of anyone or anything, so it wasn't just me. But I gave her a very wide berth the rest of our visit, walking along the cabinets to completely avoid her space.

Fortunately, for the rest of our visit, I was able to avoid Abigail. I did enjoy Mom and Dad's friends, though. Walt knew just how to rub my ears, and Zelda made sure that I got plenty of treats. I liked visiting Walt and Zelda.

And speaking of friends, I was really excited to get to meet their friends Frank and Grace. They were owned by another wheaten terrier named Erin. Erin had come to Frank and Grace directly from Ireland, and she had a different kind of coat than I did. Hers was soft and silky while mine was a bit coarser.

Mom and Dad took me with them one evening when they went to visit with Frank and Grace. It was a lovely spring day, and I enjoyed the car ride to their house. Mom put the window down for me, and I could sniff all the wonderful smells as we drove along. I was safe in the car because I had my harness hooked to the tether in the car, and Mom had special screens made for the car window so that I could enjoy the breeze but couldn't put my head out of the window.

Anyway, the drive was very pleasant; and when we got to their house, Frank and Grace were happy to meet me and were happy to have a good and proper wheaten greeting sitting quietly. After I landed, I walked over and bent down in a play bow. My butt was up in the air, but I was telling her in dog body language that I wanted to play. She returned the bow, and then we stood up and sniffed each other all over. That's the way dogs get to know things about each other.

Once we finished our greetings, we went into Frank and Grace's house. I was surprised when we kept walking straight through the house and into their backyard. Compared to our backyard at home, theirs was quite small, but they did have a swimming pool. I sniffed carefully at the edge of the pool, and Erin woofed softly that she wasn't interested in swimming. I told her that I agreed but then went on to tell her a little bit about Sulley. She said that she didn't know anything about dock diving. The only dock she knew was the one that led to the boat.

I was thinking about that when Grace came over to me and fitted a coat onto my back. I was a bit startled, thinking it was much too nice of a day to need a coat, when I looked over and saw Frank putting a coat on Erin. As I pondered that, I watched Mom and Dad coming over to me and taking my leash. We then followed Frank, Grace, and Erin down to the dock and onto their boat.

Erin quietly explained that these were special coats. She then pointed out that the humans all had things called life jackets on and these were dog life jackets. If we were to fall from the boat, the jacket would keep us afloat until someone could lift us from the water. I shook myself and said that I wasn't planning on getting wet!

With that, Dad and Frank were talking about the boat, and Mom and Grace were sitting on the bench near the back of the boat. Erin settled onto the bench next to Grace, but I was content to lie next to Mom's feet. The boat was rocking around a bit, and I wasn't feeling too steady on my feet. Erin laughed at me a little and said I'd get used to it.

After a little while, I felt the boat pick up speed, and my curiosity got the better of me. I climbed up onto the bench next to Mom and was pleasantly surprised to find that I rather liked it. There was a little taste of salt in the air, and the breezes felt good. I looked around and saw lots of new things—seagulls swooping near the boat, other boats and their people waving at us, and even a dolphin splashing alongside our boat.

Frank slowed the boat and then stopped it, and he and Dad sat on some chairs near the front of the boat and talked while they fished. Erin had gone down into the cabin of the boat, and Grace suggested we go inside as well. I was very curious to see what inside a boat looked like, so I thought that was a very good idea.

I had a little trouble on the stairs because they were more like a ladder than regular stairs, so Mom helped me down into a space that looked like a nice living room. I was surprised to see that Erin was sound asleep in a fluffy bed and hadn't noticed that we'd come in. I sniffed around a little bit, but I didn't want to be too nosy.

Meanwhile, Mom and Grace were putting together a snack platter and some drinks and took them up to Dad and Frank. On their second trip, they took some tea and a bowl of water for Erin and me.

We stayed on the boat for several hours, then headed back to their house. I had gotten used to moving around on the boat and had even figured out how to go up and down the stairs. I was glad, though, to see Frank and Grace's house because it would mean I'd be back on land soon and could make a potty stop.

After Frank docked the boat, Mom and Grace gathered the dishes that they'd used, and we all clambered onto the dock. The ground felt as though it was moving, and Mom and Dad had a bit of a laugh at my expense as I wobbled around a bit, getting used to be back on solid ground. I was just glad that I didn't fall over while I was making my potty stop!

We went inside, and the humans talked while Erin and I settled in for a nap. All of that fresh air was tiring!

Here's Duffy

I had been living with Mom and Dad for a couple of years, and we had settled into a nice routine. We often hiked on weekends. Mom and Dad went to work during the day, and I spent my days napping on the couch or on the rug in a sun puddle. Once in a while, I'd have to go see my doctor for a checkup, but I didn't mind because she always gave me tasty treats for being a good boy. We took occasional trips. Like I said, a comfortable routine.

One evening, though, when Mom got home from work, Dad put my harness on me while Mom gathered some things into a bag. I couldn't really see what she was gathering up, but she carried it out to the car. I was a bit confused because it didn't seem like a normal trip to the doctor. It was almost dark, so we were not going hiking. We seemed to drive forever, and when we stopped, Mom told me that I was going to have to wait in the car by myself for a little while. Now I was really confused. This was quite different from what we normally did in the evening. Mom reached into the bag she'd brought and gave me a couple of treats. I munched on those, then sat and looked out of the window while I waited. As she left, she mentioned that she was going to get a surprise for me. I wondered if she was going to bring cheese, or a new toy, or ice cream, or?

A puppy? A puppy! Dad lifted me out of the car and put me down on the sidewalk as Mom came out of the building carrying a puppy! I was so excited to see another pup just like me. Well, sort of like me. Wheaten terrier puppies are a caramel brown, and my coat was silvery beige. When I was a little puppy, my hair was also that beautiful caramel brown, and it changed as I got older. Now that I was around two years old, it would not be changing again.

This roly-poly puppy came trundling toward me, almost tripping over his own feet. I sat and laughed at him and then gave him some serious sniffing all over. Mom told me that his new name was Duffy and that he was going to come live with us. We were going to be his forever home.

Duffy looked at me and snorted a bit. "I'm about ten weeks old, and I've had three homes already," he said. He continued, "Four if you count the barn where I was born. What does 'forever' mean anyway?"

I thought about that for a few seconds. That meant that this little guy did not live with his mom very long after he was born. His eyes were barely open when they gave him to some new humans. That was awful! I bent down and promised him I would do my best to teach him his puppy lessons and that he would be safe. I knew my people, and they were now his people. We were a family.

Duffy looked up at me and snorted again. I knew that he didn't trust me, and he certainly didn't trust Mom and Dad yet. People hadn't been too nice to him in his short life. He didn't know how different his life was going to be now that he was part of our family. I hoped that he would give us a chance to love him. I licked Mom's hand to tell her that I was going to be the best big brother that I could be for Duffy. Mom rubbed my ears and gave us both a piece of cheese.

During the ride back to our house, Mom held Duffy in her arms. I sat next to them, and I tried to reassure Duffy that things were going to be good for him. He ignored me while he squirmed around quite a bit, and he tried to bite at Mom's arms. I was glad that she had a long-sleeved shirt on to protect her arms from his sharp puppy teeth.

Mom was gently telling him that he was not to bite, but Duffy didn't want to listen. I reached over and carefully held his neck and gave a slight growl. It wasn't a mean I'm-mad-at-you or I-don't-like-you growl but rather a listen-to-me growl. I told him to settle down and that he was not to bite Mom. Duffy was startled, but he stopped wiggling and snuggled into her arms. I don't think he really wanted to, but the movement of the car was making him sleepy. As he fell asleep, Mom smiled at me and told me I was going to be an excellent big brother.

Mom and Dad were talking as we rode home. I was paying close attention to what they were saying because I wanted to learn all about Duffy, who was now napping in Mom's arms. Mom was glad that her friend had met me when I was a puppy because that was how Linda knew that wheaten coats change so dramatically. Linda's coworker at the shelter did not think that Duffy was a wheaten, but Linda recognized the breed and called Mom.

Apparently Duffy was adopted by his first family when he was only about seven weeks old. He had eaten a few meals of mushy food, and the people who owned his mom decided that he was old enough to sell. He was scooped up with his brother and sister and put in a crate. The next thing he knew, he was in another cage in a room where there were bright lights and lots of other barking dogs. He huddled with his siblings in confusion. Later that day, his brother was taken from the crate, and Duffy never saw him again. The same thing happened when his sister disappeared, and Duffy was left all alone. He was scared, lonely, and very confused.

A day or so later, someone came in and took him from the cage. He was taken to a little room and handed to some humans. They had a people puppy, and that child grabbed Duffy and squeezed him hard. Duffy yelped, and the other people just laughed. The people talked a bit. Duffy was put in a box, and they all left the store.

Duffy's mom didn't have enough time with him to teach many of the important puppy lessons, so he did not know about proper potty behaviors. He went to the bathroom on the rug, and the man was upset. He picked up Duffy, rubbed his nose in the puddle, and put him back in his cage. After that, Duffy rarely was allowed out of the cage, and the child would grab at his ears and pull them through the cage openings. When that hurt, Duffy snapped at the child.

As a result, the adults decided that Duffy was too rough. They gave him to friends of theirs, but Duffy's life didn't get much better. These new people already had a dog, and that dog wanted nothing to do with Duffy. When he tried to talk to the other dog, that dog just growled at him, and they were the if-you-don't-leave-me-alone-you-will-regret-it kind of growls. Duffy spent his time curled up as far away from the big dog as he could get. Duffy decided that people and dogs weren't to be trusted.

About a week later, Duffy was picked up by one of the humans and put in a box. He was taken to the local dog shelter, where the kind volunteers put him into a small crate with a blanket. They put a small bowl of food and one of water in his crate with him and left him alone for a little while so that he could adjust. Duffy finally felt as though he could relax. He was all alone, but he had decided that he preferred that to being with mean people and surly dogs. It wasn't cozy, but this third home was the best so far. The volunteers would stop by and tell him how cute he was, but he wasn't listening. He didn't want to allow himself to trust them, even if they seemed like they didn't plan to hurt him.

Duffy slept that night all alone in the shelter, and the next morning, Linda came into work and met the new puppy. She knew right away that Duffy was a wheaten terrier and should be given the opportunity to go live with my Mom and Dad. Linda made a few phone calls and talked to the people at the shelter. As a result of one of those calls, Mom and Dad made the trip up to the shelter to bring Duffy home.

When I felt the car stop, I gently nudged Duffy with my nose and said, "We're home."

Duffy looked up groggily and then snorted. "Home," he said, then more to himself than to me, "I wonder what's waiting to attack me there."

My heart sank at his words, and I quietly told him that things would be different now and that he would be safe here.

Duffy looked at me very warily and then up at Mom, who gave him a gentle squeeze and said, "Welcome home, Duffy."

We stopped outside. I went potty, but Duffy didn't seem to know what to do. I thought he went potty; but I guess he didn't because, as soon as we got inside, Duffy immediately ran to the rug and went to the bathroom. He then tried to hide behind a chair. It was funny in a way because his back end and tail were hanging out, but it was also sad because he had obviously been punished for this before.

Dad went and got some paper towels to clean up, and Mom scooped him up from his hiding spot.

She rubbed his ears and said, "I'm sorry, Duffy. We should have made the stop outside a bit longer for you."

Duffy looked confused, and when he was back down on the floor, he looked over to me.

"I didn't get hit," he said with a bit of shock in his voice.

I assured him that he wouldn't get hit in this house.

"They didn't yell either," he said, trying to figure out what was going on.

He didn't seem convinced when I said that Mom and Dad didn't yell.

Mom went to fix a couple of bowls of food for us, and I was surprised to see a second crate set up next to mine. I hadn't noticed Dad doing that. I went into my crate and waited for my bowl of food, and Dad brought Duffy and put him into the new crate along with his bowl of food. Duffy dove into the food, and for the next few minutes, the only sound was that of Duffy devouring his food. I ate mine much more slowly, savoring each bite. I later learned that, in Duffy's experience before our house, food bowls were only put in the crates for a few minutes, then taken away. He had to eat as fast as he could to get as much food as he could. He had a bottle to lick from to get his water, but it was often empty. When he told me that, I assured him that there was always fresh water in two bowls in our house. He looked at me as though I was telling him a fairy tale.

When finished, Duffy simply sat quietly. Dad came over and opened both crates and ushered us outside. Duffy was too small to go down the steps, so Dad lifted him down to the grass. I smiled because I remember him doing that for me too. Duffy just sat down on the grass, unsure about what to do. I walked over to him to see if I could help him when he asked me what the stuff was that we were standing on. I suddenly realized that he had never spent time outdoors before. I was sad learning about what Duffy had and had not experienced in his short life.

After telling him about grass and dirt and patio, I tried to explain how pottying works. I described how we would come outside after we ate or when we woke up, along with other times during the day. He nodded that he understood and said that he would try. I reassured him that Mom and Dad knew that he was just a little guy and that accidents do happen. He asked me about what happened when I had an accident, and I told him that I didn't have them anymore because I was grown up.

"But if you did, what would they hit you with? Or do they just rub your nose in it?" he asked with considerable worry in his voice.

I tried again to reassure him that Mom and Dad were not like those bad people he used to live with. I don't think he was convinced yet.

I showed him around the yard a little bit. He was fascinated by all of the different smells and the feel of the different textures under his feet. After a while, Dad called us to come, so I started to run toward the deck. I stopped short when I realized Duffy didn't know what Dad meant, so I circled back and nudged him toward the house. We walked over to Dad together.

Dad rubbed my ears and said, "You're teaching him all of the things you know! Good boy!"

Dad then picked up Duffy, and we went into the house. We all settled in the TV room, and I brought a soft toy over to Duffy. It was an old one of mine that I didn't play with anymore, but I thought he might like it. I dropped it in front of Duffy, and he just looked at the toy and then at me. Duffy wasn't quite sure what to do with the toy as he shyly confided that he had never seen a toy before. I brought over a few other toys and showed him how some bounced, others had squeakers, and still others were good for chewing.

Duffy excitedly moved from toy to toy, trying each one. He settled on a soft green alligator and promptly tried to chew off the leg. I watched while he was happily chewing on the alligator, and I was really glad that I hadn't shared my Kitty with him. With that, I looked around and was relieved to see that Kitty was up on a shelf where Duffy could not reach it. Mom knew how special Kitty was to me and that I wouldn't want to share that particular toy with anyone.

As I got to know more about him, I learned that Duffy was really a great guy. He was a lot of fun to be with and was nearly always ready for a game of chase, but there were some things that frightened him that I just couldn't figure out. A lot of dogs are afraid of fireworks and thunder, but Duffy was also afraid of other things that just didn't make sense.

He didn't like funny noises or changes. He didn't like new things or changes to routine. When Dad hung some metal turtles onto the shed, Duffy had to bark at those for a while. Dad even lifted one down so that Duffy could sniff it, but he still was very wary of them. I tried awfully hard to show him that he didn't have to be afraid of those things, but I couldn't always reassure him. I tried sometimes to distract him, so I'd grab a toy and start running to get him to chase me and forget about what had frightened him. We would usually end up running into each other and laughing. We had fun, but Mom didn't like it too much if our game took us through the kitchen while she was trying to cook. Dad would try to stop us and tell us to play inside games. That would make us run even faster.

We spent most of our time together. We always went outside together, but we had different routines once out there. I preferred to go potty out by the shrubs, do what I needed to do, and then go sit by the fence to watch the world go by. Duffy liked to walk in huge circles that gradually got smaller until he found the perfect potty spot. I made the mistake once of trying to talk with him during his circles, and he growled at me because he had to start all over again. Once he was done, he'd often go off to see what he could chase. Sometimes it was a squirrel or a chipmunk; sometimes it was me. We would race around the shed and the bushes, and we could hear Mom and Dad up on the deck laughing at our antics. Other times, our race would be to see who could get to the fence first when our neighbor Robin would come over to say hi. She always had wonderful smells with her. She would reach over the fence and give us pats and ear rubs.

Once in a while, we would hear Sara at the other fence. She was a hound dog of some sort and belonged to the daughter of our other neighbors. Tina would bring Sara for visits fairly often, and we would all run along the fence barking and tail wagging and jumping. She was a lot of fun, but I was also glad to go inside and rest after her visits. She was younger even than Duffy and had a lot of energy.

I think the best times I spent with Duffy were when we would cuddle together. I loved feeling him next to me because it reminded me of my puppy brothers and sisters back at Cam's when I still lived there with Cam and my dog mom, Morgan. Duffy said he just liked the feeling of security that he got when he leaned against me. I didn't think he believed me when I told him stories about my time with Cam and Morgan. Duffy shared a small crate with his brother and sister before they went to the store to be sold. They didn't get to snuggle with their mom; they only got to see her when it was time to eat. I cannot imagine how horrible that must have been for such a young puppy.

We also got to snuggle at bedtime, when we would both climb up onto the big bed with Mom and Dad. I always snuggled between them, and Mom would put her arm around me. That was so nice and cozy! Duffy preferred sleeping at the foot of the bed and would usually lie on top of Dad's feet. I tried that once or twice, but I never slept very well at that spot. I was always afraid that I would get kicked. Looking back on it now, those snuggles on the bed were the best of times—all four of us together.

I was trying my best to teach Duffy the puppy lessons that he had not had time to learn from his mom, but I knew that I couldn't teach him everything that he needed to know. I was relieved when I heard Dad say that Duffy would be going to puppy classes to learn the basics. For the next few weeks, either Mom or Dad would leave with Duffy for a few hours one evening, and he attended his school. Each week, he would come home and tell me about the things that he had learned; and throughout the week, we would practice his lessons.

Over the coming weeks, Duffy did quite well at his lessons, both the classes at his puppy school and the lessons I was teaching him. I was a bit disappointed for Duffy when he did not pass his Canine Good Citizen test, but I knew that he just did not like it when he could not see anyone from his family. When he got home that night, he was sad and concerned.

"I screwed up," he said. "I didn't pass the test."

I assured him that he could always ask for another chance to take the test. He sounded a bit relieved about that and then admitted that he was concerned about how Mom and Dad felt. I assured him that they were disappointed for him but not disappointed in him, and that was an important distinction. Duffy wondered aloud if this would mean he would be going to another house. I growled at him and informed him that, if anyone was going to take him anywhere, they were going to have to deal with me! I then barked more gently to him to reassure him that he was part of our family and he wasn't going anywhere.

After Duffy passed his regular puppy-school classes, I was surprised a few weeks later when Mom told me that we were both going to go to my old trainer for some more classes. I was looking forward to seeing Joe and showing him that I remembered my lessons from my puppy classes. When we got to Joe's school and went into his training room, Joe looked up from the papers he was holding and called my name. I hesitated briefly, then realized that Mom had unclipped my leash, so I ran over to him, with my tail wagging happily. I liked Joe, and it was good to see him again.

When I reached him, I sat down at once, just as he had taught me to do. He was happy to see that I remembered my lessons. He then motioned to Mom to unclip Duffy's leash, and he called Duffy to him. Duffy came flying over to us and stopped about two feet away. He then cautiously approached Joe. Joe gently gave Duffy some pets, and Duffy visibly relaxed. I realized then that Duffy had never approached Joe when he wasn't on his leash before, so this was a different situation for him to figure out.

Once classes started, Joe made sure that he worked with both of us, individually and as a team. We both learned the same commands for certain things. For example, "come," we both knew that we were to stop doing whatever we were doing and run as fast as we could straight to Mom and Dad. He also taught us some new commands that were very similar. If Dad said "here," I learned that was my command to come just me by myself. Duffy wasn't to listen to that command. At the same time, Duffy's special command was "place!"

That meant Duffy was to go running to Dad while I stayed in place. It was hard, but eventually we learned.

Other commands required that we work together. I knew how to hike with Mom and Dad, but Duffy hadn't been exposed to hiking yet. The night we worked on trail hiking, Mom and Dad brought their hiking poles. We learned that we were supposed to walk right in front of Mom or Dad, mostly in front of their left leg. That kept us safely out of the way of their poles.

We learned that, if Mom or Dad said "hike close," we were to move closer to them and stay about three feet in front of them. Another new command was "trail off." That command meant we were to move all of the way to the right side of the trail as far to the right as we could. That one didn't make any sense to us until we were actually hiking a few weeks later and a group of bicycles came up and passed us on the left. They came so fast that they startled us, and it was good we were far away from them.

Graduating from Joe's classes was exciting because it meant that we were ready to go on some longer and more interesting hikes. I tried to describe hiking to Duffy, but he just couldn't picture what I was telling him.

He got to experience hiking firsthand a few weeks later. Early one Saturday morning, a week or two after we graduated from Joe's classes, I saw Mom filling some little bottles with water. She also gathered some treats into baggies, and as I followed her into the dining room, I saw our packs on the table. I watched her put the treats and water bottles into our packs and then looked past her into the kitchen, where Dad was putting water into their water bottles. He added some people treats into their backpacks, so I knew that we were going to be going on a longer hike than our recent walks around the neighborhood. Those had been nice, and it had given Duffy the chance to learn about wearing a pack. I was looking forward to having the chance to go out on a real hike.

After getting everything together, Dad carried all the backpacks, hiking poles, and hiking leashes into the Jeep. Duffy and I hopped into the back seat, and Mom and Dad clipped our harnesses into the seat belts. Once we were underway, I sat and looked out of the window while Duffy tried to climb into the front seat with Mom. He didn't really mind riding in the car, but he would have preferred being in the front seat. Mom finally convinced him to sit down and relax. He sat, but I can't say that he exactly relaxed.

When Dad pulled into the parking lot, I recognized that we were at the same park where we had gone for my first hike. Once the car stopped, Mom came around and carefully put my pack onto me, clipping all of the straps and snapping on my hiking leash.

Meanwhile, Dad was trying to do the same for Duffy. Once Duffy smelled all of the wonderful new smells at the park, he completely forgot all his lessons! He wanted to run and jump and smell everything. Dad laughed and said that it was like trying to put a backpack onto a bag of Jell-O! Dad finally got Duffy strapped into his backpack and clipped to his hiking leash and then put his own backpack.

We started down one of the trails, and Duffy darted from left to right. As he started to get a little tired, he gradually slowed down and started to remember his lessons. We walked a while at a comfortable pace, and we saw a few other hikers as we went along the trail. We came to a small bridge, and Mom and Dad decided it was a good time to take a break. Dad reached into my pack and took out a small silicon bowl and a bottle of water from Duffy's pack. Duffy and I shared a drink of water, and then Mom gave us some treats. Naturally, after eating something, Duffy needed a potty break. He was a little uncomfortable doing his business while on the leash, but he finally finished his circles and did what he needed to do. Mom used a plastic bag from Duffy's pack to pick up his poop, and after tying the bag closed, she put it into Duffy's pack.

"Carry in. Carry out," she said, which meant that she wouldn't leave a mess behind.

We walked for a while longer, then the decision was made to walk back to the car. We took another break for more water and treats and then went back to the Jeep. Once back at the Jeep, Mom and Dad took our packs off, and we clipped into the seat belts for the ride home. As we rode home, Duffy kept asking me if I saw this or smelled that. He was so excited! I really wanted to take a nap, but

Duffy's excited woofs and yips kept me from falling asleep. I couldn't blame him, though, because I remember how exciting my first hike was.

Most Saturday mornings, weather permitting of course, since I didn't like hiking in the rain, we could be found hiking one of the trails within a short drive from our house. Once in a while, we would travel a bit longer for our hikes, and those were extra enjoyable because we would often sniff lots of exotic smells. I could always tell when we were going for a longer hike because Mom would put extra treats in our packs.

So understandably I was a little confused one Saturday when I saw Mom putting our hiking bowls and water bottles into one of her canvas shopping bags. Duffy was happy to see that she remembered to put treats into her bag as we sat and watched their preparations. We were going somewhere—that was obvious—but we couldn't figure out where we were going. Dad brought our car harnesses and carefully buckled the clips and attached our regular walking leashes.

He teased Duffy a little because he had to adjust a couple of Duffy's straps; his harness was getting a little snug. "You might have to switch from the tasty treats to green beans, Duffy. You're putting on a little weight!"

Duffy looked at me with a worried expression, and I explained that Dad was just having some fun. I'm not certain that Duffy believed me, but he did relax a little.

Anyway, we went out to the car, hopped in, and clipped into the seat belts; and off we went. As usual, Duffy used his paw to try to convince Mom to let him up into the front seat, and I sat quietly looking out of the window. Duffy didn't get to move to the front seat, and I decided to take a nap after a while. I woke up when I felt Dad parking the car in front of a huge building that I had never seen before. Duffy and I were both very curious about this place.

As soon as the car doors opened, we could see and smell lots of other dogs, and there were hundreds of people walking about. I could smell hamburgers in the distance, along with some other treats and goodies. We walked over to a small patch of grass, and I reminded Duffy to do his business. We both felt better after that potty stop, we walked nicely on our leashes into the building. As Mom and Dad paid for our entry into this special show, I caught a faint whiff of a familiar scent. I tried to puzzle what it was. It smelled comforting and familiar, and yet I could not quite place it in my memory.

We walked into this giant room that was filled with many, many people. Some were walking with their dogs; others were moving about without any dogs. Still others were standing in what looked like pens with their own toys. Those people seemed to want to share their toys with the people not in pens. I know that we stopped at a couple of places, and Mom and Dad talked to the people about scissors and some lotion for Duffy's allergies. Once again, I caught a brief sniff of that oddly familiar scent. I was truly puzzled. I would have liked to have been allowed to go track the scent to try to find it, but I knew that I wouldn't be allowed off of my leash.

We walked around the huge room admiring the latest in collars and beds and crates and toys. I especially liked the treat booths because, many times, the people in those pens offered samples to Duffy and me. I always remembered to sit up straight and take the treat gently. Duffy was not quite as refined, but he tried. Some of the treats were incredibly good. Others reminded me of cardboard.

Suddenly I smelled that familiar smell again, and it was much stronger and closer. I turned around in time to see Mom hugging another human, and I realized it was Denise! I saw Dad and Jim shaking hands, and my eyes followed the leash that Jim was holding down toward a beautiful little girl wheaten.

"Molly June?" I woofed quietly.

Molly June turned, and with an excited pounce and lots of wiggles, she came running to me. We sniffed and sniffed and woofed and whined. We had so much to tell each other. Somewhere in the middle of that, Duffy barked loudly.

"Oh, Molly June, this is my brother, Duffy," I said as I introduced them.

Molly June laughed and woofed. Another extremely cute little wheaten girl walked over and shyly stood there. Molly June introduced us to Lily Rose, her sister. While the humans chatted, we caught up, and I learned of all of Molly June's adventures. Our talk turned back to Cam and Morgan, and while we had both heard stories about our puppy siblings, we had not heard of any others who had had nose-to-nose visits.

Mom and Dad suggested to Jim and Denise that we walk over to the food area and sit and chat a bit more. Duffy liked the idea when he heard food, but Molly June and I were just glad that we would have more time to talk. While the people talked, Duffy gently begged for treats. Lily Rose sat and watched the crowds go by, and Molly June and I sat together, leaning on each other and catching up on the events from the past couple of years. We were so happy to see each other that Molly even forgot to ask for extra treats!

After a while, our people decided that it was time us to all move along. Denise wanted to investigate some of the training resources, and Jim laughingly reminded everyone that Molly June needed to find a few treat stations. Duffy asked Lily Rose if she knew about treat stations, and she chuckled as she nodded. She said that Molly June had a treat station in every room! Anyway, as we parted, Molly June and I reluctantly said goodbye but took heart in knowing that we really did live close enough to each other that we might see one another again.

Duffy spent much of the ride home teasing me about my girlfriend. He knew some of the stories from my time with Cam and Morgan, but I didn't want to describe too much about Molly June and my other brothers and sisters. I knew my early months were so different from his time with his mom, and I did not want to make him sad. He must have realized a bit about the stark differences because he fell quiet and whimpered some on the ride home. I snuggled next to him to try to comfort him, and I licked his paw until he fell asleep. Mom commented again that I was being a good big brother to Duffy.

After Duffy fell asleep, I thought again about how good my life was. I had plenty of food, warm beds, a yard to play in, and a brother to play with. It had been wonderful to see Molly June and hear about her life with Denise and Jim and to meet her sister, Lily Rose. As I snuggled with Duffy and reminisced, the gentle movement of the car lulled me into a nap. As I drifted off to sleep, though, I wondered what our next adventure would be.

Ouch!

Duffy and I were inseparable, and I spent my days trying to be a good big brother and teaching him how to be a good wheaten terrier. One day, though, Duffy had to be the strong one and take care of me for a while. We had been playing tag in the backyard, and I ran into a lawn ornament. It was nearly dusk, and with the fading light and the shadows, I did not see this glass ball hanging from a hook out near the woods. I was running full speed after Duffy when I ran into the ball.

Mom later said she heard the crack when I hit the ball and thought that I had crashed through a bush. It was only when she saw Duffy pushing me toward the house that she realized something was wrong. As we got closer, she could see the huge red spot forming on my back, and she ran inside. I was upset that she ran away, and Duffy got mad. He helped me up onto the deck and was about to give Mom a piece of his mind when she came back holding a towel. She looked closely at my back and put the towel over the wound. She then took an elastic bandage and tightly wrapped it around the towel and my chest. It was tight enough to feel like a hug and to put pressure on my cut, but it did not keep me from being able to breathe.

We all went inside, and Mom called Dr. Barbara, my veterinarian. No one had looked at the clock, and Mom later realized that Dr. Barbara must have stayed late that evening for some reason because her office normally would have been closed at that time. Dr. Barbara told us to come on over. She would wait for us.

Mom and Dad grabbed their going-away-from-the-house things—wallets, keys, and phones. Duffy stood back out of the way. He didn't like changes in routine, and this was certainly a change in routine! Mom took a minute and knelt down next to him to thank him for helping me. She rubbed his ears a little and gave him an extra-special treat. Duffy woofed at me to ask how I was feeling, and I quietly woofed that I was in pain and I was really tired. He told me that Dr. Barbara would help me feel better and that he would try extra hard to be good while everyone was at the doctor's even though he didn't like being left alone.

Dad lifted me into the car but did not put my harness or anything on me. I didn't feel like running anywhere; I just wanted to have my back stop hurting. I put my head on Mom's shoulder while she was driving and licked her ear. I wanted her to know that I was sorry for messing up whatever evening plans she might have had. She reached back and rubbed my nose a little.

"You're a good boy, Quincy. I'm sorry that I left that lawn thing where you could get hurt on it," she said softly.

We got to Dr. Barbara's office. She took one look at my bandage and my gums, and she gave me a shot of something to make the pain go away. She could tell that I was in pain by looking at how I was standing, and the color of my gums told her I was going into shock. Shock is the body's reaction to a significant injury, and blood flow slows down. This can hurt the insides of the patient, so it's really important that it be treated as quickly as possible.

Dr. Barbara made a call to the emergency veterinarian to tell them that she was having me come to them for treatment. She didn't even take the bandage off to look at my back! She did tell Mom that she had done an excellent job on the bandage. It was exactly the right kind of pressure on my back to keep it from bleeding more. We left Dr. Barbara's office, and Mom raced to the emergency veterinarian. When we got there, Mom went inside while Dad was lifting me out of the car. Several of their technicians met Dad, took me in their arms, and whisked me away to the doctors.

I didn't like that they made Mom and Dad stay in the other room when they carried me back to see the doctors. Dr. Armen let Cam stay with us, and Dr. Barbara never made them leave either. I started to grumble a bit, and that was when the doctors put a muzzle on me! The nice technician told me that it was to protect everyone and that the doctors would be able to relax and do their jobs better if I wore the muzzle for a little while. I didn't like it but decided that it was probably for the best. After they fitted the muzzle, several people supported me as they weighed me. Knowing how much I weighed would help make sure that I received the correct amount of medicine.

Next the technicians carefully lifted me up and gently put me on a table. They carefully cut away the bandage that Mom had put on my back. One of the doctors commented on what a respectable job was done on the bandage and that it helped stop my back from bleeding. That made me feel better because they said the same things that Dr. Barbara had said. I trusted her, and this helped me trust them too.

Once the bandage was removed, the doctors realized just how deep and how long the cut was, and things started to happen very quickly. One technician carefully shaved my front leg and gently slipped in a needle. I barely felt the needle, and as he did that, he explained to me that they would give me medicine through that needle instead of having to poke me a bunch of times. I liked that idea. I was beginning to sense that there could be a lot of pokes over the next few hours.

While they were getting the needle positioned in my leg, another technician gently shaved my back. The buzzing of the clippers felt funny, and I was glad when that was done. It didn't exactly tickle, nor did it hurt. But I didn't like the sensation. Once they had finished that, they used some clean water to wash the dirt and debris from my back. I heard a technician comment that they would have to do more once I was asleep. I guessed that meant I was going to have to stay at the hospital for a while. Once they felt the big pieces of dirt were washed away, they put a new bandage on my back. This one had some medicine on it to help reduce the chances of an infection.

Someone else carefully removed my collar and carried it out to where Mom and Dad were waiting. They explained that it was best for Mom and Dad to have it so that it did not get misplaced. The technician also told Mom and Dad that they would be called into one of the exam rooms to talk to the doctor in a little while so that they could get an update on what they had done and what the next steps would be.

Mom looked at the collar in her hand and said, "I bet Quincy's upset that they took his collar off. He doesn't like to be without it."

She didn't know it, but that was exactly what I was thinking back in the examination room. I felt naked without my collar!

Meanwhile, the technician took a bag of fluid and hung it on a hook near the table. True to his word, the technician attached the tube from that bag to the needle in my front leg and let the liquid slowly drip. I later overheard Mom and Dad telling one of their friends that the emergency vet had given me fluids to keep me from becoming dehydrated. Another technician came over and added some medicine to make me relax. As much as I wanted to watch everything that was going on, I started to get very sleepy, so I closed my eyes for a brief nap.

While I was napping, a technician called Mom and Dad into an empty examination room, and the doctor met them there. He told Mom that she had done an excellent job bandaging my back and that she probably saved my life. He told them that they had given me fluids and that I was napping comfortably since they gave me some pain medicine. He went on to tell them that they had flushed some of the dirt out of the wound and that they had put a fresh bandage on with some medicine to keep it clean and to start the healing.

The doctor also explained that they had put a muzzle on me. They had used a soft muzzle, a simple tube of fabric that went over my nose and mouth to keep me from being able to open my mouth too far. This was part of their routine procedure, and it was done to protect everyone. Dogs tend to snap and bite when they are afraid or if they are hurt, so the muzzle keeps their patients from doing that. Mom and Dad knew that I would never bite anyone, but they understood the precaution was necessary. The doctors didn't know me as well as they did.

The doctor then explained that I was going to need to have surgery to close the wound. While I was asleep for the surgery, he would be able to really clean the area, and he would need to put in a lot of stitches. The doctor admitted that he was amazed at my injury.

Even though it was a deep cut and an awfully long cut, nothing inside of me was hurt too badly. He emphasized that it was a bad injury, but it could have been much, much worse. He then explained that, because it was such a deep cut, he would have to insert several drains that would gather the extra fluid that accumulates during healing. Again he assured Mom and Dad that this was normal procedures.

Mom and Dad told the doctor to go ahead and do the surgery. They also knew that I would have to be in the hospital at least three days. They asked if they could see me before they went home, and since I was sleeping on a rolling bed, the doctor asked the technician to roll me into the room with Mom and Dad. They were upset to see how tired I looked but relieved that I did not appear to be in pain. They each gave me a hug, and Mom kissed my nose.

She leaned in closely and whispered in my ear, "Get better, Quincy. We love you."

I sort of remember hearing them, but I was so sleepy that I couldn't reply, not even with a little tail wag. Mom and Dad thanked the doctor for the information and then left the hospital to go home to Duffy.

Duffy told me later that it was very upsetting for him when they came home without me. He ran around behind them to see if I was hiding. He sniffed my collar and then sat and looked up at them with questions in his eyes. Mom knelt down and hugged him extra tightly. She explained that I was going to have to stay at the hospital for a couple of days so that the doctors could fix the cut on my back.

Dad sat down in his chair and called Duffy over to him. Duffy looked really sad. I know he felt that my injury was somehow his fault, and I'm glad that Dad tried to make him feel better. He called Duffy over and had Duffy put his paws on his chest. They hugged each other.

Dad said, "I know you're worried about Quincy. We all are, but we'll just have to wait now until he can come back home."

Duffy wagged his tail slowly to let Dad know that he understood, but he couldn't shake the guilty feelings. Mom came over and sat next to them and put her hand on Duffy's back.

"Duffy, this wasn't your fault. It wasn't Quincy's fault. It was an accident," she said.

She then added that she would check the yard the next day to make sure that there weren't any other hazards where we liked to play.

Duffy joined Mom and Dad on the big bed for some cuddles but hopped down off of the bed later that night. He went over to my crate and crawled into my bed to sleep. He told me that he wanted to smell my smells and it would help him think good thoughts for me. He admitted that he tried licking my bed since that seemed to comfort me, but it didn't work for him. All it did was make his tongue feel fuzzy! He went and found one of our squeaky toys that no longer had a squeak and chewed on that until he fell asleep. His last thought as he drifted off was that he missed me and hoped that I'd be home soon. When he told me that a few days later, it made me feel incredibly special.

At the hospital the next morning, my day started early. The technicians moved me from the hospital crate onto the rolling bed and then to an examination room. In that room, they took my temperature, measured my blood pressure, weighed me again, and even took a little bit of my blood to run some tests on it. Satisfied that I was ready for surgery, they rolled me into the operating room. Once I was there, they transferred me onto the operating table. That table was cold! It was also extremely hard. I remember thinking that I didn't mind sleeping on the hard floor at home, but I didn't like this hard bed very much in the hospital.

While I was thinking about the cold, hard bed, the technicians got everything ready for my surgery. This included getting the tools ready for the surgeon and the bandages all in place for after the surgery and preparing me for the operation. The first thing they did was give me some more medicine through my front leg to help me relax, and then they held a special cone over my nose. The air from the cone smelled a little funny, but before I could decide what it smelled like, I drifted off to sleep. To help me breathe while I was sleeping, they put a special tube in my throat and another little tube in my nose. The doctors took really good care of me.

During the operation, they carefully checked everywhere inside the cut for any little bits of dirt, glass, or metal. They knew what they were looking for because they had asked Mom what I had hit. They made sure to get everything extra clean and then started to close the wound. The cut was so long and so deep that they had to put some stitches deep into my back while others were just on top, closing the skin. They also put the drains in and held them in place with stitches on the inside and tape on the outside. When they were finished, I had nearly forty stitches from my collar to my tail. The technicians then put a yellow net sweater over me to keep everything in place. It certainly wasn't fashionable, but it worked to keep the drains from dangling and to keep the bandages in position.

After surgery, the technicians put me back on the rolling bed and took me to my hospital crate. I don't remember being moved back into that crate, only waking up a while later. It took me a few minutes to remember where I was and why. I shifted position a little and then noticed the sweater and could feel the bandages. The technicians were pleased to see that I was waking up and brought me a tiny bit of water. A little later, they offered me some food. But that really didn't smell all that good to me, so I refused it. They took it away and tried again later. I didn't like the smell of it then either. But I was hungry, so I ate some of it. Meanwhile, one of the technicians called Mom and Dad and told them that the surgery had gone well and that they could come see me the next evening. The doctors wanted me to have a full day of rest before seeing Mom and Dad.

Mom and Dad came to see me the next evening. They waited anxiously in the visiting room and jumped up a bit when the technician led me as I walked slowly into the room. I was sore and a bit cranky, so I just stood with my head down and my tail down. I didn't want to look up at Mom and Dad in part because it hurt to lift my head to look up. Thinking back, I'm not sure if I was hurting as much as I just wanted to go home. Everyone was taking diligent care of me; but I wanted to go home to my own bed, my own food, and my own family. I know that it wasn't fair to Mom and Dad, but I spent a lot of time during their visit whimpering. I know that I made them feel bad too, but I couldn't help it. I was miserable, and I was trying to let everyone else know just how miserable I felt.

My days in the hospital were boring. I had to stay in my hospital crate, and my crate was in a room with other dogs that were recovering. The way the room was set up, I really couldn't see much of what was going on, so I just napped and rested most of the time. Well, I rested in between the times the staff came in to check my temperature, blood pressure, and heart rate. They would come in to give me water and bits of that yucky food. I didn't mind the company, and it helped pass the time.

I was still very sore and a bit weak from my surgery, so when it was time for me to go out for a potty trip, the technicians would lift me from my crate. I enjoyed those times, though, because I could look around and see what else was happening. Once I could go outside, I appreciated sniffing the different smells. I was trying to remember them all so that I could tell Duffy about them.

After a full day of rest and another sleep at the hospital, I was a little surprised when they took me into a work room and removed the sweater and the bandages. The doctor came in, looked at everything, and then put on a fresh bandage and sweater. I overheard him tell the technician that I was cleared for discharge and that they should call my Mom and Dad to come get me. I was so excited, but when I tried to wag my tail to say thank you, I discovered that movement pulled on my stitches. I told myself that I'd have to remember that when I saw Mom and Dad. It was hard to wait for Mom and Dad to come. Each time I heard the door open or close, I'd turn to see if they were coming for me; and most of those times, I was disappointed.

Finally, the technician came to get me. She set down the bag she had and carefully tied the straps, securing a huge clear cone around my neck. I knew the cone was to keep me from bothering my wound, but it was extremely ugly and uncomfortable. I knew exactly why it was called the "cone of shame." She then picked up the bag, and we walked slowly to the visiting room. I liked that she slowed her pace to match mine.

She paused and bent down to rub my ears. "I've enjoyed meeting you, Quincy. I'm glad you're feeling better, and you'll get stronger and stronger as you heal. Pretty soon, you'll be running as fast as you ever did."

I felt better hearing that. I would have liked to know when I could get rid of that cone, but she didn't tell me.

We went into the visiting room, and the technician waited patiently as Mom gently fastened my collar around my neck. She kept it loose so that it didn't bother my bandages, but she could tell how much better I felt just with that simple gesture—one more step closer to normal. The technician then gave Mom the bag and explained that my follow-up instructions and medications were in the bag. The technician then showed Mom and Dad how to clean my drains. Dad left for a few minutes and came back with a card reminder for my next appointment. We said goodbye to everyone there and made our way out to the car. Dad lifted me into the back, and we started for home. I was so happy to sniff all those familiar smells in the car.

When we got home, Mom came around to the back of the car and gently loosened the straps on the cone. She said that she knew that had to be uncomfortable, so she had come up with a different solution. On their way to pick me up, they went at the drugstore and bought two soft foam collars. These soft collars were the ones that humans used if they hurt their necks, but Mom had the idea to put two of those together so that I wouldn't have to wear that awful cone of shame. She used some soft fabric tape to stack them together, and much to my relief, it worked! I couldn't get to my stitches or drains to lick or scratch anything, but I didn't have that huge cone to bump into things. I also discovered that, with Mom's invention, I could eat and drink on my own and didn't have to wait to have the cone removed. My mom was so smart!

After Dad lifted me from the car, I walked very slowly to the front door. I was excited to be there and looking forward to seeing Duffy and taking a nap in my own crate. As I climbed the steps onto the front porch, I could hear Duffy barking, but it sounded as though he was far away. That didn't seem right. I expected him to be right on the other side of the door when we walked in. What I didn't know was that Mom and Dad had put Duffy into his crate so that he couldn't jump on me when I first got home. They knew that we were both excited to see each other, so they put him into his crate so that he couldn't bump into my back on our initial meeting. When Dad let Duffy out of his crate, Mom held onto his collar so that he could sniff my back and my bandages and everything but he couldn't accidentally hurt me. Once he sniffed everything and we woofed to each other a little, he understood that he would have to take it easy with me for a little while until my back healed completely.

I went into my crate to rest, and Duffy came and stretched out with his nose to my crate door. It was comforting to have him close by, and I was glad that he was there. I had missed him while I was in the hospital, and it was obvious that he had missed me. We talked a bit about my experience in the hospital before I drifted off to sleep. Duffy rolled over and put his back against the door of my crate. He wasn't going to let me go anywhere without him knowing about it.

Mom took over my medical routine now that I was home. Each morning, she had to clean out the drains that were in my back. They were designed to allow the extra fluids to collect and not make a mess. This was all part of the normal healing process, but it was time consuming since I had four drains. She also had to make sure that the bandages were affixed properly and that everything looked as though it was healing properly. She also had to give me my medicine. I didn't make that easy for her unfortunately.

I need to make a confession. I have always hated taking pills, even those "yummy" heartworm pills that are supposed to be delicious. I would resist every pill that was given to me. Unfortunately, though, in order to heal from my injury, I was expected to take a whole pharmacy's worth of pills. Several of them were huge! Mom got a special syringe and would gently push the pills down my throat that way. It did not hurt, and it kept me from spitting out the pills. I guess it was a win for everyone, but I still hated pills. She would always give me an extra-special treat once I'd taken all of my pills. That made it almost tolerable.

It seemed to take a long time for my back to get completely better. The day after I came home from the hospital, Mom and I went to see Dr. Barbara. She had my medical records from the hospital, but she wanted to see how I was doing. She commented that she knew that it was serious the night when Mom called because Mom sounded upset. Everyone in Dr. Barbara's office was glad to see me, and they gave me lots of treats. I was glad to see everyone too because I really liked them all. Dr. Barbara watched Mom clean out one of my drains and said that she was following the procedure perfectly. Mom was glad to hear that.

A few days later, we went back up to the hospital for them to check everything. The technician came and took me into the back. While I was off visiting with the staff—and getting my bandages changed—the doctor told Mom and Dad a bit more about my injury and just how close I had come to doing some severe damage. Mom assured her that all of the similar hazards had been removed. The doctor then told them what a good patient I was and that I was so friendly. I felt good when Dad later told me that they had gotten a good report card on me!

I had to go back to the doctor again in another week. On that visit, they removed the bandages but left the yellow sweater on since I still had all my drains. Everything was healing as it should, and they were pleased with how Mom and Dad were taking care of my wound. It was starting to itch, but Mom's invention was making it impossible for me to scratch it. I asked Duffy if he'd scratch it for me, but he just looked at me as though I was crazy. Mom talked to Dr. Barbara for an idea to make things less itchy, and she suggested that Mom put some special cream on it to keep the skin from getting so dry. That helped a lot, and I was much more comfortable.

Finally, about four weeks after my accident, we went back to the doctor; and he removed the drains! He put some little bandages over the places where the drains had been but told Mom she could take them off in a day or so. He also told us that I didn't have to wear the yellow net sweater anymore. I still had to take a bunch of pills, but Mom made sure that I took them all until I finished each of the medicines.

By then, the hair on my back had started to grow back in, but the hair grew back in a different color! The new hair over the scar on my back was the same caramel brown that my hair was when I was a little puppy. Dad called it wound hair and said that was perfectly normal for a wheaten terrier. At first, I was embarrassed because it looked different and other people asked about it. I sometimes got extra treats when people found out how badly I was hurt, and that was a little embarrassing too. If Duffy was around, he would always sit next to me to get a treat too. Little brothers can be a bit pesky at times. Anyway, eventually my hair color returned to normal, and no one could really tell where I was hurt. That took a long time—about a year, as I recall.

Another thing that took a while for me was to get used to running around in the backyard. I knew that Mom had already removed the yard decorations that were like the one that hurt me, but I was still sort of afraid that I would run into something again and get hurt. The first time that I went into the yard after all my bandages were gone, I was very, very careful. I remembered how badly it hurt when I was first injured and how much Mom and Dad worried. I didn't want to have any of us go through that experience again.

In the beginning, I was happy to just walk around in the yard, sniffing all of the interesting things to sniff. When I passed by some of the bushes, their leaves brushed my back, and it sort of tickled where my hair was so short. Mom had me wear my coat some days because the weather was getting colder, and she didn't want me to be too cold. Even though wheaten terriers love the cold, I liked wearing my coat. It felt sort of like a hug from Mom when I put it on. Mom made Duffy wear his coat on the same days that I had to. He grumbled about it, though, saying that, just because she thought that I was cold, it didn't mean that he was too. We both admitted, though, that we were pretty lucky to have coats and warm beds. We heard stories of too many other dogs that did not have those things.

Duffy kept pestering me to play. He would run over and pretend that he was going to hit me, then turn just before he did, trying to entice me to play. I wanted to play, but I was just afraid. I tried to explain that to Duffy, but I think it frustrated him. Gradually I got increasingly comfortable running in the yard. Finally, one day, I surprised him by chasing after him when he came over to annoy me and tease me to get me to chase him. After our game ended, he came over to me and said that he was really glad that I agreed to play. He had been afraid that I was mad at him for playing chase with him the night I got hurt. He thought I might have still blamed him for my injury. I gave him a playful bump and said that I had never blamed him. It was an accident, and accidents just happen sometimes. I then challenged him to a race to the deck, where I knew Dad was waiting with cookies.

I was ahead of Duffy when we got to the deck, but he beat me when he took a flying leap up the steps. Dad and I both laughed at him when he landed and skidded across the deck, having forgotten about the wet leaves. He picked himself up, shook off a few leaves, and calmly walked over to the door. As much as he tried to pretend that he had planned his landing that way, I knew otherwise.

Walking through the door to go inside, Duffy whispered to me that he was glad I was feeling better. I told him that I was glad too and suggested that we go into the TV room for a nap. He challenged me to a race, but I told him I was tired and I'd meet him there. Abandoning the race, we walked together down the hall and snuggled together on the big dog bed on the floor. At last, things were getting back to normal.

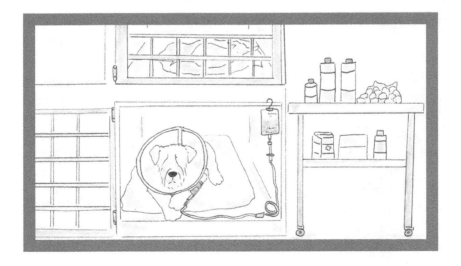

Where Are We Going Now?

One day, about a year or so after my accident, I saw Mom get out a large duffel bag. I guessed that meant that they were going to go away in the car for a long time, at least a few days. This made me sad because I knew that I would miss them while they were away. I really liked our dog sitter, Vicki, but I knew that I would still miss Mom and Dad. Duffy didn't realize what was going on because he hadn't been paying attention. He came over and nudged me to ask why I was looking sad. I told him that Mom and Dad were leaving us for a while. He looked shocked and started to follow Dad around the house, not letting him out of his sight.

Meanwhile, as I watched Mom put their things into that large bag, I saw her take out a smaller bag. I decided to follow her as she put a couple of bowls, leashes, some papers, and a container of treats into that bag. Then she opened our big food container and scooped out meal-sized portions into small plastic bags. She then put those food bags into the bag with the bowls. Slowly it came to me—we were all going on a trip together. We hadn't taken a trip all together since Duffy came to live with us, so I had forgotten that possibility. I told Duffy of this alternative idea, but I don't think it made him feel any better. Since he'd never gone on a long trip before, he didn't know what I meant.

Early the next morning, Dad took our crates apart and put them into the back of the car. He then took their duffel bag and the smaller bag and put them in the back as well. He also moved some other bags that I hadn't seen before to the car. They looked as though they were filled with towels and our regular hiking backpacks and even some of our combs and brushes! Meanwhile, Mom was fastening our harnesses securely and clipping a leash to each of us. Duffy looked at me with questions in his eyes as we walked out to the car and hopped in. Mom attached our harnesses to the seat belts, and we were off! We just didn't know where we were going.

After a while, Duffy leaned over to me and said, "I guess you were right. We are all traveling together."

We were in the car forever. We stopped every so often to have a short walk, but we were basically riding in the car for a full day. Duffy and I took turns looking out of the windows, and as usual Duffy tried to get into the front seat with Mom and Dad. I don't know why he kept trying; he was never going to be successful as long as he was clipped into the retaining strap in the back of the car.

Eventually we pulled up in front of a very tall building, and Dad went inside. After a short time, he came back out and told us that everything was set up. Again Duffy and I were confused. What was there to be set up? Dad parked the car, and we gathered everything together. Mom held our leashes while Dad put our crates onto a cart and then put the other bags into the crates. Once everything was loaded onto the cart, we started toward the building. Mom walked slightly ahead of the cart holding our leashes while Dad followed pushing the cart.

After a short walk, we came to a door. Mom opened the door, held it for Dad, and told us to stay out of the way. After he'd pushed the cart through the opening, we walked alongside Mom into a long hallway. From there, we stopped in front of some shiny metal doors. The stone floor in front of those metal doors was very cool on my feet! Mom pushed a button, and after a couple of minutes, the shiny doors opened. I could see this tiny room. Dad went in first with the cart and our crates, then Mom followed with Duffy and me. Dad pushed a button, and with a jerk, it felt as though the entire room was moving!

The moving room came to a stop with another bit of a jerk. The doors opened, and we walked out into another hallway. We walked slowly down the hall until Mom did something and opened the door to another room. This was a more normally sized room, but it was still very odd. It was like a bedroom, but there were no other rooms to explore. I remembered the motel room that we stayed in when we visited Mom when she was on her trip for work, but this place didn't have the extra room. It didn't have a kitchen. That worried Duffy quite a bit, but I reminded him that Mom had packed food for us. Meanwhile, Dad set up our crates and then told us to go to our rooms. We ran to our familiar spaces, and we settled in quickly. They gave us some treats and left us in the room. It was dark and cool, so we both settled in for a nap. As I drifted off to sleep, I wondered where we were—and why.

Mom and Dad came back to the room a little later and invited us out of our rooms. We both jumped up on the bed with them and enjoyed a bit of gentle roughhousing with Dad. Meanwhile, Mom had put our dinners into our bowls and refilled our water bowl. Traveling can make one very hungry! We enjoyed our dinner, rode in the room with the shiny doors again, and took a quick walk outside for a potty trip. Once done, we came back up to our room.

Mom said something to Dad about the hotel being very nice and that we had handled the elevator very well. I thought about that a little and realized that the place I had stayed with Mom and Dad was called a motel, and since it was all one floor, it didn't need an elevator. This hotel was tall, so we needed the elevator to get up to our floor. The room had two beds, and Mom moved the pillows to relax on one while Dad had already stretched out on the other. We waited to be invited up onto the beds; but once invited, without exchanging any words, Duffy jumped up and leaned against Dad while I stretched out with Mom.

We were all wonderfully comfortable. I don't remember falling asleep that night, but I do remember how contented and happy I felt as I snuggled next to Mom. I could hear both Duffy and Dad snoring on the other bed.

Mom woke up first the next morning, and after getting dressed, she walked out the back door of the room. I hadn't noticed that door the night before, so I quietly followed her. I was startled to discover that the backyard here was only a few feet wide and that I couldn't get to the grass. I sat down to think about this a little when Mom reached over and rubbed my ears a little. She explained that this was a balcony and that we could sit and watch the sunrise over the ocean. I sat next to her and listened to the new sounds. There was something that was making a rushing and roaring sound. Noisy birds screeched nearby, and I could hear the cars moving down the road. Meanwhile, the air smelled delicious. It was sort of salty and incredibly fresh. I took many deep breaths trying to capture as much of this fresh air as I could.

After a little while, Duffy and Dad joined us on the balcony. I tried to explain to Duffy what Mom had told me, but he was a little frightened by the distance to the ground. We really were high up! He chose to sit behind Dad's chair. From there, he couldn't see the ocean below, but he could still smell the fresh sea breezes.

Suddenly there was a knock at the other door. Duffy forgot his fear and started to run toward the door to bark, but Dad called him back and told him to sit. Duffy listened and came back, this time sitting next to Dad's chair. Mom had gotten up and gone to the door, and she pushed the door to the balcony closed as she did. Dad, Duffy, and I sat there and looked out over the ocean and waited to see what was going on.

Mom went to go see who it was and came back a few minutes later with a small cart with goodies on it. Dad commented that he had not realized that she had ordered something called room service. I didn't think that it looked much like a room. It looked like food to me, but if that's what he wanted to call it, it was fine with me as long as I got some! Dad was happy to have his mug of coffee, and Mom sipped her tea as they munched on some pastries and toast. Mom then lifted a silver cover from another plate on the tray and carefully cut the food into two portions. I thought it was odd that she only ordered one of the plates, but that mystery was solved when slid some of the food onto one of the other plates from the tray and put one plate in front of Duffy and one in front of me.

We both happily devoured the scrambled eggs before us. I was delighted to discover cheese mixed in with the eggs and contentedly licked my chops when I was done eating. Duffy continued to lick the plate until I was concerned that he was going to lick the design from the plate! If this was all part of vacation, I would be happy to have a vacation every day. Once everyone had finished eaten, Dad gathered the plates and put them back on the cart. He moved the cart closer to the door we used when we originally entered the room. He then called us all into the room and pushed the door closed. He told Mom that he didn't want to leave us on the balcony without supervision to keep us safe.

After they got dressed, Mom asked Dad to put our harnesses on while she got her pack ready. While Dad put our harnesses onto us, we watched Mom put some bottles of water and water bowls into her pack. She added a couple of small towels and then announced that she was ready to go.

Mom held our leashes while Dad pushed the breakfast cart into the hall. Mom and Dad took our leashes, and we went down the hall and then into the moving room, which I now knew was called an elevator. As before, the floor jerked a bit as we both started down, and then when we came to a stop, the doors slid open. Once again, we stepped out onto the cool stone floor. I turned toward the entry we had used when we first arrived, but Mom gently tugged on my leash to tell me that we were going in a different direction.

As we walked, there were so many things to see that I felt as though my head was on a swivel. After a short walk, we went out a side door, then turned and walked a sidewalk along the building. I could see the end of the sidewalk and wondered where we would be going once the pavement ended.

We came to the end of the sidewalk, and Mom and Dad kept walking. This wasn't grass! It was soft and squishy. It was also hard to walk on. I noticed that Mom and Dad had taken off their shoes and were walking barefoot in the sand. It wasn't easy for them either, which made me feel a little better. After a short walk between some sand hills, we came to a stop. I heard Mom take a deep breath.

"It feels so good to be here at the beach again."

It wasn't "again" for me, but I agreed that it felt good!

Mom turned to Dad and suggested that we all go for a walk before settling down at the umbrella. I didn't know what she meant by settling at the umbrella, but a walk did sound like a nice idea. We continued to walk closer and closer to the ocean. I was surprised because Duffy was the first to run toward the waves and the first to run back when the waves came toward him. The sand was firmer closer to the water. It was much easier to walk, but I didn't want to get wet from the waves. I was glad that Dad had Duffy's leash and that Mom had mine, so I didn't have to stay next to him all the time. As we walked farther, Duffy started enthusiastically chasing the waves and jumping into them while Mom and I walked right along the water's edge staying as dry as possible.

We walked for a long time, with everyone taking turns getting their feet wet and splashing in the water. I was even willing to get my feet wet after a while. I was glad that Mom had brought our water dish and a few bottles of water with her. I tasted the ocean water, and it was just too salty! After a while, Mom and Dad decided that we had walked far enough, and we turned around and headed back to the hotel.

Once we got close to our hotel, I noticed that there were chairs and umbrellas lined up in the sand. Mom and I went over to talk with a person I hadn't seen before, so I made sure to behave my absolute best. I was happy when he climbed down from his very tall chair to say hello to me, and I very gently wagged my tail in greeting. Mom talked with him for a few minutes, and then he walked over to one of the umbrellas and pinned a note to it. Mom told Dad that this was their spot for the week. Duffy was a little disappointed that he hadn't gotten the chance to say hi to the lifeguard, but Dad assured him that there would be time for that later.

Mom reached into her backpack again and pulled out a mat. She spread it over the sand and told Duffy and me that we could lie there and we wouldn't get so sandy. I was happy for the chance to rest, but Duffy wanted to be up and looking around a bit longer. Dad settled into one of the chairs, and I soon heard him softly snoring. I saw that Mom had a book with her, but she wasn't really reading. Instead she was simply watching the ocean and listening to the seabirds squawk overhead. She looked a little sad, so I moved to rest my head on her leg.

She reached down and rubbed my ears. "Thanks, Quincy. I love being here at the beach, but it brings back a bunch of memories. Some of those make me a little sad."

She then picked up her book to read, and I settled on the mat next to Duffy. I could not believe how relaxing it was on the beach.

We relaxed under our beach umbrella for a while, and then Dad left for a bit. Duffy stood up to watch where he went, but he soon lost sight of him when he walked between the sand dunes. After short time, Dad came back with a bag; and once he got to our umbrella, we learned that it had some hot dogs, potato chips, and drinks for Mom and him. Mom and Dad ate their lunch. It was hard to behave, but Duffy and I sat quietly next to them. Duffy nudged Dad a couple of times to remind him that we were there, but Dad ignored him.

We were surprised to learn then that the bag had a few more hot dogs and a couple of water bottles left in it once they had finished eating. Mom took a couple of paper plates and carefully tore the hot dogs into pieces and put the plates onto the mat, one for Duffy and one for me. I guess it was the walk and the salt air that had made me so hungry, but I devoured that hot dog in record time. Even Duffy commented that he had never seen me eat something so quickly! Mom put fresh water into our bowls, and after a drink, everyone settled to watch the waves and the people.

A couple of times during our time on the beach, either Mom or Dad would get up from their chair and walk down to the ocean. The first time, I was amazed to watch Mom keep walking right into the water and to keep going until she was in the water up to her neck! I was worried, and I kept looking up at Dad to see if he was worried. I tugged at my leash—we needed to go save her! It was about then that I saw her walking back up out of the water and toward us. I took a huge sigh of relief. She grabbed one of the small towels and wiped her face.

"The water is delightful," she said to Dad.

He got up and walked toward the water, saying, "My turn!" as he went.

I don't know how long we were on the sandy beach, but sometime after lunch, Mom and Dad decided it was time for us to go back to the room. They gathered all our belongings back into Mom's backpack and then did a final check to make sure that all of the trash had been thrown away. She confirmed that she had our water bowls and blanket, and we started back up through the soft sand toward the sidewalk. I was relieved when we came to the sidewalk and the ground was firmer. Walking through the sand made my legs really tired!

We walked a short distance on the sidewalk, then veered off to the left a little. I hadn't noticed the hose and table when we walked down to the beach, but apparently Mom had. She set everything down on a table and then picked up the hose that was attached at the side of the building. She rinsed the sand from her legs and then sprayed Dad's feet and legs. I eyed her warily as I was not interested in getting a shower. She carefully washed each of my feet but said that she wasn't giving me a bath right then. Duffy, on the other hand, received much more rinsing than I did because he had chosen to lie in the sand and not on the mat that Mom had brought for us. He grumbled that, if he had realized that a bath would follow, he might not have had as much fun earlier in the day.

Another trip in the elevator and we were soon back at our room. Mom took our mat and went out on the balcony. She shook it well, then laid it on the floor of the balcony to get dry. She rinsed our bowls to get rid of the sand and then took Duffy into the bathroom. Based on the noises I could hear, he was getting a complete and proper bath! It slowly dawned on me that Dad hadn't removed my leash and that he wasn't letting me up on the bed, so I started to suspect my bath was next. Sure enough, once Duffy's bath was done, Mom took me into the bathroom; and it was my turn. I noticed that she was extra careful to rinse between my toes, making sure that the sand was gone so that my feet wouldn't get sore. I wouldn't tell Duffy, but I thought the bath felt nice after being outside in the warm air all day.

After we both had our baths, Mom and Dad told us to go to our crates for a rest. I can't speak for Duffy, but I know that I was happy to relax in my little room. It did not take long for me to fall asleep. Just as I drifted off, I could hear Duffy's snores coming from his room next to me. Mom and Dad took their showers, got dressed, and quietly left the room and went for their dinner. I wasn't worried. I knew that they would come back, and we would enjoy our dinner and then cuddles for the evening.

We followed this pattern for the rest of the week with a few minor changes here and there as Mom and Dad would sometimes do something in the afternoons, leaving Duffy and me in our crates. I honestly didn't mind because it was a chance to rest and to talk with Duffy. We laughed and talked like best friends do and completely enjoyed our vacation time together.

One morning, I saw Mom gathering everything into the duffel bags again. I guessed that we were going to be heading home again, and when Dad took apart our crates, I was quite sure that I was right. He announced that he was taking them down to the car and came back up after a few minutes. Mom had finished packing everything else by then, so he carried those things downstairs. Mom took a final look around the room, and then we walked down the elevator to ride down and meet up with Dad. He brushed the last of the sand from our feet as we got into the car, and he hooked our harnesses into the seat belts again. I was a little sad to be leaving the hotel but knew that Duffy and I would share our memories from the trip for a long time. We both agreed that we liked the beach.

Dad stopped to put gas in the car before we really got started, and then we pulled out and onto a big highway. The ride was uneventful, and I alternated between looking out the window and napping. As usual, Duffy kept trying to climb into the front seat with Mom, and I would hear her yelp from time to time when Duffy's toenails scraped her arm. He was extremely persistent and continued to try to convince her that he should be up front. I kept telling him that he wasn't going to win that argument, but he countered that it was always worth trying.

We stopped midafternoon in front of a long, low building. When I looked around, I was a little confused. It did not look like a rest area, with all of the cars and trucks and hurrying people. It did not look like a regular gas station, with cars and trucks and that yucky gasoline smell. It wasn't another hotel, and it didn't look like the motel that I stayed in before. It wasn't home, and it didn't really look like anyone else's house that I'd seen either. I sat and watched as Dad left us all in the car and go into the building. He came back a brief time later, triumphantly waving a card at Mom. He got back into the car and drove to the other end of the building. He parked, and both Mom and Dad got out of the car.

Mom carried the duffel bags into the room while Dad carried our crates inside. Whatever this place was, we would be staying here for at least a little while. Dad put our crates together while Mom took us over to a grassy patch for us to go potty. It took us both a little longer than usual because there were lots of interesting smells to sniff. Mom finally got bored and told us to come along. We obediently trotted along with her back to the room.

As we went into the room, I realized that this was another motel but a smaller one. Like the hotel, we didn't have a kitchen; but like the other motel, we didn't need the elevator. Just like before, the room had two beds, and Dad had already claimed one for himself. Duffy hopped up next to him, and they were contentedly flipping through the channels on the television. Mom was standing by the front window, where she had thoughtfully opened the curtains just a bit so I could look outside, talking to someone on her phone.

Her call finished, and she said to Dad, "They will be here in about twenty minutes."

I wondered who they were and hoped that they were friendly.

Sure enough, about twenty minutes later, there was a knock at the door. I had forgotten about Mom's phone call at first and initially thought it was a bit odd for us to be having our eggs at this time of day. Imagine my surprise when the door opened and two people came into the room and enveloped Mom and Dad with hugs. I sniffed the air and remembered that scent from somewhere. I was just trying to remember where when another scent hit my nose. This one was even more familiar, and it was then that I saw the pup walking with them. That extra scent was my brother Sulley! We had many excited woofs and sniffs and tail wags when I heard a quiet woof off to the side. I apologized to Duffy and explained that this was my brother Sulley. Duffy and Sulley sniffed each other politely, and we three settled in to visit a bit while Mom, Dad, Mike, and Sherry talked.

Sulley explained that his people were on their own vacation and we all happened to be in the same city at the same time.

Mike and Sherry had brought a folding crate into our room for Sulley and set it up so that we were all close enough to talk. We three pups went into our rooms. Mom dropped a few treats into each crate and then left to have dinner with Mike, Sherry, and Dad. Sulley and I shared stories of our lives since we'd left Cam's house, where we were born, and Duffy tried to tell Sulley about all the silly things I'd done. We had a wonderful evening.

I was sad when Mike and Sherry had to leave, taking Sulley with them. It had been great to be able to spend a few hours with my brother, and it was wonderful to hear how much he loved his home in Florida, complete with his very own swimming pool. His stories about going out on the boat with Mike sounded like a lot of fun as well. Those tales reminded me about my trip on the boat with Frank, Grace, and Erin.

I was just a little sad, though, because remembering the good times with Sulley and my other brothers and sisters highlighted for Duffy how different his time with his mom had been and what he had missed. I tried to cuddle with him a bit more than usual that evening, but I could tell he was sad. I also sensed he was just a bit angry with the humans that had torn his family apart. Reminding him that he was safe in our family seemed to help, but I could tell he was still upset. I really wished I could erase those bad memories and bad feelings for Duffy, but those were things that he would have to work out on his own. I know that his close relationship with Dad helped because Dad would sometimes tell Duffy about some of his own bad memories and hug Duffy to thank him for listening. Duffy would talk to Dad in his own way, and Dad would gently pet Duffy to let him know that he understood.

The next morning, after a good night's sleep, Mom and Dad put all our things into the car one last time; and we continued the drive home. I will admit I was starting to miss home even though this had been a wonderful vacation. I sort of wanted to get back to our normal routine. I especially wanted to be able to run freely like I could in our backyard.

We stopped a couple of times on the rest of the drive home, just as we had on the other legs of our trip. I didn't mind the rest-area stops because they had grass and interesting smells, but I really didn't care for gas-station stops. We weren't allowed out of the car at those, and they had that yucky gasoline smell. I understood that we needed those stops so that we could put fuel in the car, but that didn't make me like them any better.

Mom and Dad made quick stops for their meals while we were traveling. They didn't want to leave us alone in the car, so they would talk through the window to some people at the windows of their buildings and ask for food. Mom always reminded Dad to get food for us. I don't know if he really forgot that we were with him or if he was just teasing Mom. It didn't matter in the long run, though, because we always got something tasty to eat, like chicken bits or a plain hamburger. Yum!

Dad would always get the bag of food, and then we would pull over to the side in the parking lot to eat. Mom and Dad would always eat first, making sure our food became cool enough for us to safely eat it. Mom would also tear our food into smaller bits so that we wouldn't eat it too fast. It also made it easier for us to eat. When we were done, Mom and Dad would clip on our leashes and take us for a short potty walk. I felt funny having them so close. I hated that they had to pick up after us, but Mom explained it was the right thing to do.

After our dinner that day and after riding for a little while longer, I suddenly heard a sound I recognized. My head popped up, and my thoughts were confirmed. We were nearly home. The smells were familiar. The sights were familiar, and we soon felt the bumpy bumps as we turned into the driveway. Everyone climbed out of the car and stretched. Mom took Duffy and me through the side gate and then unbuckled our harnesses. It felt so good to run with my legs fully extended and to feel the cool grass between my toes.

Meanwhile, Dad had carried our crates into the house and wiped the last bits of sand from them. He fluffed our crate pads, and everything was put back in its proper place. Mom refilled our water bowls and then called us to come inside. Duffy flew up the steps onto the deck and pushed past Dad. He ran a few zoomies up and down the hall, showing how happy he was to be home, and then we all settled down in the TV room until it was time for bed. Once settled in our usual sleeping spots on the big bed, I sighed a huge sigh of contentment. Vacation was nice, but being home again was even nicer.

That didn't mean that I didn't enjoy our trips. About a year later, I was napping peacefully on the sofa in the living room when Duffy came racing down the hallway. He leapt onto the couch, startling me awake. He excitedly told me that he saw Dad putting some things into a duffel bag and that there were little packets of our food on the dining room table. In Duffy's mind, this meant that we were going to go on some sort of trip with Mom and Dad. I yawned and stretched a bit, then hopped down to casually wander past Dad to see what I could figure out.

Dad saw me coming toward him and jokingly said "Oh, so you're up. Just in time to move to the car and take another nap."

My ears perked up with that comment. Duffy was right, and we were going to go somewhere with Mom and Dad. I further surmised that it was going to be a trip lasting several days since Dad had a small pile of food packets in front of him on the table.

What had me puzzled, though, was that he had already carried our things out to the car and Mom wasn't home from work yet. Dad always did get home first, but he rarely did anything other than cook dinner before Mom got home. He was packing and not fixing dinner. This was highly unusual.

A bit later, Mom got home from work and went into the bedroom to change into jeans. She then gathered a few things and added them to the duffel bag that Dad had started to fill.

"Did you get toothbrushes? Shampoo? Vitamins?"

She seemed to have some sort of mental checklist that she was referencing and was pleased when Dad said yes to everything.

"Do you have the dogs' food? Bowls?"

Again another of Mom's checklists, and again Dad had everything.

Mom carried another small bag out to the car while Dad moved the duffel bag to the side in the cargo area. I knew he was doing that so that Duffy and I would have plenty of space to nap. The very last thing that they carried out to the car looked to be a gift box of some sort. Now I was extra curious about where we were headed.

We rode along for a while, and then Dad stopped the car. While Mom waited in the car with us, Dad went inside and came back in a few minutes carrying a bag with some delicious-smelling food. As usual, Mom and Dad ate their dinner first, and then Mom carefully tore apart our hamburgers and put them into our traveling food bowls. She tore the burgers into small pieces so that we didn't eat too fast.

I thought the burger was delicious and turned to ask Duffy what he thought. I didn't have to ask, though, because his bowl was already completely empty; and Duffy was licking it to get every last bit of flavor from the bowl. I turned back to my dinner and finished it with a few more mouthfuls. Dad then clipped our leashes onto us, and Mom rinsed our food bowls with a bit of water. She then put some water into the bowls to offer to us. Duffy slurped his water noisily while I took much more refined sips. Dad walked us over to some grass and gave us a few minutes to go potty. He cleaned up after us, tossing the waste bags into a trash can, and we all got back into the car and buckled in. I settled in for another nap while Duffy moved to the front of the cargo area to see if he could convince Mom to let him into the front seat. She wasn't convinced, so he finally settled down and stretched out next to me.

It was dark when the car stopped again—very dark because there were no streetlights or other houses nearby. Mom got out of the car first, and I saw another person walking quickly to meet her. They chatted excitedly for a few minutes, and then Dad got out of the car. By now, there was another man standing next to the woman, and Dad greeted them both. He came around to the back of the car and lifted out the duffel bag while Mom clipped on our leashes. Mom walked us over to a patch of grass, and we both pottied. After a quick cleanup, we all walked into the house.

It was then that I realized I'd met one of these people before. I remembered her smells from the time Mom and I met her for lunch. I started to wag my tail.

Mom commented to her friend, "Deb, I believe Quincy remembers you!"

Duffy was over meeting Deb's husband, Bob, and they both seemed to enjoy the meeting. I sat like a gentleman and accepted the ear rubs from Deb. I also shyly kissed her hand.

Mom and Deb settled in at the table, talking well into the night. Dad and Bob retired to the living room and watched several movies. Duffy stretched out on the floor next to Dad. Whenever Duffy was uncertain about things, he would look to Dad for reassurance. Since this was a new place to Duffy, he wanted the comfort of being close to Dad.

Meanwhile, I was happiest with Mom. I listened to their voices and their laughter, and every now and then, Deb would slip me a piece of cheese. I felt right at home and hoped Duffy would be able to relax a bit as well.

The next morning, Bob offered to take Dad on a tour of their land. Dad was more than willing and asked Bob if Duffy and I could come along. Bob was happy for us to join them, but we had to wear our new coats. I didn't think it was that cold, but for the opportunity to walk with Dad and smell new smells, I could wear a coat.

I was surprised to see that both of our coats were the same. They were bright orange, and they matched the hats that Dad and Bob both wore. Hunter orange, Dad called it. I hoped that did not mean that we were expected to hunt anything. I soon learned that we were wearing the orange so that a hunter did not mistake us for an animal to be hunted. I was glad that everyone was taking the precautions necessary to keep us safe.

The walk through the woods was wonderful. There were all kinds of smells to sniff and places to explore. We didn't need to worry about any animals getting too close to us. Duffy was crashing through the underbrush, making enough noise for five dogs! Still it was wonderful to have the opportunity to explore.

When we got back to the house, there were more wonderful smells to enjoy. While we were out for our walk, Deb and Mom had been preparing lunch. Homemade soup and bread were on the menu, and both Duffy and I were excited to have some of the beef broth poured over some of our kibble as a treat.

We spent the afternoon in the comfort of their home, relaxing and unwinding. Bob and Deb lived out in the country quite a distance from town, so there was plenty of peace and quiet. Mom and Deb continued to visit while Dad and Bob resumed their movie marathon. I could tell that Mom and Dad were really enjoying this relaxing weekend, and I was glad to see them loving their time in the quiet countryside with their friends.

Late Sunday afternoon came, and with that, Dad loaded our things back into the car. I was a little disappointed that we had to go back home and the busyness there but was thankful we'd had this break. As we were getting ready to leave, Bob gave us both ear rubs, and I again gave Deb a few kisses. Deb also tucked a loaf of fresh bread into our bags. I could see why they were such special friends of Mom and Dad and hoped that we would plan another trip to see them again sometime soon.

Snacks and Goodies and Treats, Oh My!

Whenever our conversations turned to food, Duffy always mentioned the tasty bits of fish or the other treats Mom and Dad brought back from their dinners. I didn't share Duffy's enthusiasm for the seafood, but I did remember how terrific some of the steak pieces were. It is worth mentioning that Duffy would eat nearly anything that was put in front of him. I sort of wonder if his less-than-discriminating tastes were the result of his early days in the cages, but I never would have asked him. I was never hungry, or at least not like Duffy was before he came to our house, and I've always been a bit of a picky eater.

One time, Mom thought she was giving me a treat when she put some cut-up shrimp in my dinner bowl. I tried one piece and then politely stacked the rest of the pieces just outside of my bowl. Mom laughed when she picked up my bowl and saw the shrimp there. She said it was the same sort of thing that a little human kid would do, hiding the unwanted vegetables under their bowl. I shrugged. Other fish were tolerable, but I simply didn't like shrimp.

Duffy, on the other hand, would eat almost anything. He was absolutely crazy for bananas. I liked them well enough, but eventually Dad learned that he needed to cut up an extra banana for Duffy so that he could enjoy his own in peace. Cheese was my favorite human food, but I usually had to share that with someone. Duffy got his own banana, all to himself.

Anyway, when Duffy first came to live with us, Mom and Dad were a little worried about how possessive Duffy was of his food bowl. As I said before, Duffy was often hungry before he joined our family, so I think he guarded his dinner bowl so carefully because he remembered those times. He wanted to make sure that he got all of his food before someone took it away.

We talked about his food fears. Duffy admitted that he knew that Mom and Dad would never leave him hungry, but there was just something that made him growl if someone tried to take his bowl away or to get between him and something he wanted.

Mom and Dad knew that Duffy had had it rough, but they were not going to tolerate his growling. They made sure that we always understood that they were in charge and that we were to give them whatever we had if they asked for it. This was something that they had learned during my training classes with Joe. The logic was simple. If we became conditioned to drop whatever it was that we had when they told us to, they could use that command to protect us from something that could be dangerous. A similar command was "leave it." They used that command for things that we hadn't gotten into our mouths yet!

When we took our Good Citizen test, one of the tests was to walk down a path where there were lots of delicious cookies. We were to ignore the cookies and to keep walking to the end of the path. While walking, I started toward a cheese treat.

Mom said, "Leave it."

I looked up at her like she was crazy but kept walking. There were several along the path, and I looked at her each time, hoping that one of those times she would tell me I could have the cookie. I didn't get one until the test was completely finished!

That was another activity where Duffy had trouble with the Canine Good Citizen test. He slurped up three cookies before Dad could even say Duffy! Duffy later told me that the cheese cookies smelled better than they tasted, but I think he was just trying to make me feel better because I hadn't gotten any of them.

Anyway, because Duffy was so possessive of his dinner bowl, Mom and Dad would separate us for mealtime. They would fix our bowls in the kitchen, then call us and tell us to go to our rooms. Duffy and I would happily run into our crates, turn around, and then sit for our bowls to be placed in with us.

Every so often, Mom or Dad would put the bowl down, then say "leave it" as they took the bowl away again. I was startled the first time that they did it to me. Duffy was quite upset the first time they took his bowl away, but he got a little better with practice.

Unfortunately, there were a few treats that we simply couldn't have. Before Duffy came to live with us, once in a while, Dad would give me an elk antler to chew. I really enjoyed chewing on them. When I was done, my teeth would feel clean, and I liked the taste. Mom and Dad would let me chew one until it was about one paw wide. They would take it away then, telling me that they didn't want me to try to swallow it.

Duffy didn't want them to take it away even if it was for his own good, and he would get really mean if anyone reached for it. He would bare his teeth, growl low in his throat, put his ears back, and generally be quite menacing. Mom and Dad didn't tolerate that behavior, so they carefully removed the antler and told him to go to his crate. By then, Duffy had calmed enough that he was willing to leave his prize on the floor, and Mom picked it up. Several months passed before Duffy commented to me that we hadn't had any antlers for a while. I woofed a harmless lie and told him that I hadn't noticed. I suggested that maybe they had gotten too expensive, never letting on that I overheard Mom telling Dad that they wouldn't buy any more elk antlers because of how possessive Duffy was with his. I was a little disappointed but decided that it was for the best if it kept Duffy out of trouble.

One day, Mom came to us and told us that we were going to a luau! We both got quite excited and danced around the living room while Mom and Dad put our harnesses on. Neither of us knew what a luau was, but the way Mom said it, it had to be something good.

Once we were buckled into the car in our harnesses, I leaned against the door and let the fresh air blow the hair from my eyes and the good smells into my nose. Duffy, of course, was doing everything he could to climb into the front seat with Mom and Dad. Some things never change.

Anyway, after a short ride, we pulled into a parking lot. We looked around, and I said to Duffy that it looked as though we might be stopping to get some treats to take to the luau. I recognized that we were in the parking lot where some friends of ours had a special bakery just for dogs. Chloe and Chance were golden retrievers, and their people had opened this store so that everyone could give their pups healthy and tasty treats. Mom and Dad first met Gregg and Melissa several years before when they were making their treats in their kitchen and selling them at craft shows. We were now at their big store that had treats, toys, foods, and lots of people to get ear rubs from.

Before Mom let us out of the car, she paused and put shirts on us. Shirts? We rarely wore clothes other than our winter coats, and it certainly wasn't winter. I looked over at Dad and realized he had a brightly colored flowered shirt and that it was similar to the one that Mom had on. I looked at Duffy and saw that his shirt was flowered too and asked him what my shirt looked like.

"Huh? Oh, kind of like Mom's but a different color."

I started to wonder if flowered shirts were mandatory for a luau.

We hopped out of the car and walked over to the dog bakery. The instant the door opened, I realized that the luau was at the store! Chance wandered over to say hi, and I saw that he also had a flowered shirt on. Chloe had a funny-looking grass skirt on and a big flower tucked by her ear. Duffy and I looked around, and most of the dog guests and many of the humans had flowered shirts. Very interesting.

Duffy pointed out that Gregg had put a few trees into his store. I walked over to sniff them and realized that they were fake trees. Melissa came over and rubbed my ears a little and asked me if I liked their palm trees. I looked at her and wagged my tail a little. I wasn't quite sure how to respond to her question.

I was glad when Gregg came over and invited me to join the group over at the cake table. I happily led Mom over to the table and sat properly while Melissa's mom cut the cake. All of the dogs in attendance got a piece of delicious apple cinnamon cake with yogurt icing. Gregg is an excellent baker! All their treats and cakes are made with human ingredients, so Mom and Dad could have had a piece too.

While munching on my cake, I heard Gregg say that this was the fifth anniversary of their store's opening. Now I understood why they were hosting the luau. It was a way to say thank you to all the dogs and their people who helped them meet this important milestone.

After I finished my cake, I saw that Dad had walked Duffy over to the other side of the store so that he was alone to eat his cake. I was proud of Dad for thinking of a way to keep Duffy out of trouble, and I was happy and relieved that Duffy had managed to stay out of trouble! Mom picked up Duffy's plate and asked Dad if we should be allowed to pick out something to take home. I looked over my shoulder toward the cake, but I quickly realized that Mom meant a toy.

Duffy immediately grabbed a ball with a handle. He loved to chase those in the backyard. I looked around and found a snake with a bunch of squeakers. That's my kind of toy! I liked to squeak the squeakers until I drove either Mom or Dad crazy.

Mom and Dad congratulated Gregg and Melissa again on their store's milestone, and we gathered our treats and toys and headed home. On the way, Duffy and I agreed that a luau was a fun way to spend the afternoon, especially since it included some of Gregg's delicious cake.

I can't say that I was a perfect pup, but I generally stayed out of trouble. There were a few exceptions—for example, the time I almost got into serious trouble when we were visiting Mom and Dad's friends Frank and Grace. This happened before Duffy came to live with us. Erin and I had played together, and Erin decided that it was time for naps. I looked around and spotted a comfy sun puddle in the living room, and while Erin went to her little bed nearly tucked behind the piano, I stretched out on the rug in the sun.

I happily listened to the murmur of conversation at the dinner table and drifted off to a nap. After a bit, I awoke and looked over at the dinner table, and no one was at the table. I looked over at Erin's bed, where she was snoring contentedly. That made me feel a little better, but I was concerned about Mom and Dad. Where had they gone?

I got up, stretched, and walked toward the kitchen. From there, I could hear laughter coming from the back deck. I started to walk that direction when I caught a whiff of a delicious smell. Curiosity got the better of me, and I walked over and put my paws on the dining room table to figure out the source of that wonderful smell.

I was pleasantly surprised to find a small dish containing a creamy white sauce to be the source. I happily started licking the contents of the bowl and nearly jumped out of my skin when I heard someone call my name! Mom stood in the doorway with her hands on her hips looking quite stern.

I quickly took my nose out of the bowl and dropped my front feet back onto the floor. I tried my best to look innocent, but there was a blob of sour cream on the end of my nose. Mom tried to scold me, but I could also tell she was trying not to laugh. Grace came and stood beside her and also had trouble containing her laughter.

I was worried that I might never be invited back to Grace and Frank's house, but that wasn't the case. I did notice, though, that, on subsequent visits, the sour cream was always near the center of the table, far from my reach.

Duffy led me into trouble one time, and we were both really, really lucky that we didn't get hurt. Dad had opened the back door, and we ran out for our usual potty break and to play in the cool morning air.

Suddenly Duffy spotted something very different in our yard nestled under one of the bushes. He cautiously approached it, then woofed softly to see what this strange creature would do. I glanced over to see that Dad was moving a few deck chairs around and that he wasn't really paying attention to us.

The creature turned its head to look at the source of the woof and suddenly scrambled to its feet. Both Duffy and I were startled as this spindly-legged creature stood, looked at us, and then took off running.

Neither Duffy nor I could resist that terrier instinct to chase, so we ran after it, barking as we went. Dad looked up to see what the commotion was just in time to see us all crash through the fence gate. We continued to chase the interloper until we suddenly came to a stop in another yard.

Standing there was Jake, a huge German shorthaired pointer, who was sniffing the strange animal. Duffy and I were looking at Jake, wondering how he felt about two wheaten terriers in his yard. Just then, Mom and Dad arrived and grabbed our collars. As they paused to catch their breath, we all heard a bit of rustling off to the side and a funny little bleating noise. With that, the strange critter ran off in the direction of the noise.

Mom looked over and said that the mom deer must have heard her baby calling and came to see what was going on. The doe then called to her fawn, and the baby left to rejoin her. Jake sat down and looked at us curiously, and his owner came over to our little group. Mom and Dad clipped leashes onto our collars, and Dad started to walk back across the street to inspect the gate.

Mom and Jake's dad talked for a few minutes, then she led us back home. Once we had crossed the street, she made us sit down. She told us that the street was dangerous and that cars did not watch for dogs. If we had been hit by a car, it would have hurt a lot even more than when my back was cut. She sternly told us that we were to never cross the street without her there. We nodded our heads, but we both wondered if we would be able to behave if we saw another deer.

By then, Dad had finished checking the gate and determined that the latch had not been hooked correctly. Mom and Dad talked a bit and figured out a way to make the gate a bit more secure. As we all walked back to the deck, Mom commented to Dad that, even as well-behaved as we were, like most terriers, we couldn't be trusted off leash. The instinct to chase was just too strong. Dad commented that he was glad Jake was there and that we stopped. Who knew how far we would have run in pursuit of the fawn?

Later that afternoon, Duffy and I were standing on the couch, looking out of the front windows. We could still see Jake patrolling his yard when a car suddenly drove by our house. I could tell that it was moving very quickly. I realized then how lucky we had been earlier in the day that there were no cars on the street when we ran crazily across the street while chasing the fawn. I instantly understood why Mom had given us that lecture and resolved to try as hard as I could to never run across the street. I decided that I would stay in our backyard unless I was wearing a leash.

A Dog Named Kitty?

One night, when I was about five years old, I noticed that Dad was reading stuff on his computer. It was very unusual when he called Mom over to look at something. She looked over his shoulder for a few minutes, then she went over to her computer. I could hear her furiously typing all sorts of things. She came back to where Dad was sitting and told him that the application was in. I wondered what they were applying for, but I couldn't imagine what it could possibly be.

Off and on over the next couple of days, Dad would ask Mom if she had heard anything yet. The answer was always no. They both looked sad. Duffy and I tried to cheer them up, but there was still a hint of sadness around the house. We guessed it was about the application, but since we didn't know what they had applied for, we weren't really sure. We wondered when they would finally hear something about the application, either good news or bad.

About five days after putting in the application and just as they were getting back home from dinner with friends, Duffy and I could hear Mom and Dad talking outside.

I heard her say to Dad, "We're going to Maryland tomorrow!"

I could tell that they were excited, but neither Duffy nor I knew exactly why. We weren't even sure what a Maryland was. We were simply happy to hear that they were happy.

They came on into the house and got our dinners ready for us. While we ate, Mom and Dad scurried around the house putting things into a bag. It reminded me a little of the bag that Cam sent home with me when Mom and Dad adopted me a long time ago, and I hoped that it didn't mean that Duffy was leaving. I was quite sure that I wasn't going anywhere because I remembered Mom's promise that she would love me forever. I had assumed that she had made the same promise to Duffy, but I wasn't positive about that.

Duffy finished his dinner and came and sat with me as I finished mine. I've always eaten more slowly than Duffy, preferring to savor the flavors. Together we watched Mom and Dad gather a leash, some treats, some bottles of water, and a bowl and put them into the bag. With each item, it seemed even more like the bag that Cam sent home with me. Duffy asked me if I had any ideas about why they were gathering all those things. I didn't want to mention the similarity to my bag, so I asked him if Mom had ever made any promises to him.

He looked down at the ground and said, "She told me that she would love me forever. I didn't believe her at the time, and I sort of growled at her. I do believe her now, but I don't know how to ask her to forgive me for growling."

I nudged him and assured him that I was confident that she knew why he had growled and that she probably didn't even remember it now.

He sighed and said, "I hope so."

It was just about then that Mom came over to where we were, and she put her arms around both of us. She gave us each a big hug, kissed our noses, and told us that they would be back home in a little while. Duffy and I looked with confusion but decided that they would tell us what was going on when they got back.

Mom and Dad were gone for a couple of hours, and during that time, Duffy and I tried to guess what was going on. I told Duffy about the bag that I had when I first came to live with Mom and Dad and that the things that they put in the bag were remarkably similar. Duffy looked alarmed and wondered out loud if either of us were going to be sent away. As he asked that awful question, I realized that the collar that Dad had put in the bag was one of our puppy collars and that it would never fit Duffy or me. I pointed that out to Duffy, and we both felt a wave of relief. This meant that the bag that Mom and Dad put together most likely was not a bag for either of us.

Meanwhile, Mom and Dad were at a big store. They had had to drive a bit farther away to find a store that was open so late at night. They wandered the aisles gathering a few things for our family but also a collection of things that were on their special shopping list for the evening.

Specifically, they bought another collar. It was a puppy-sized collar, and it was pink. They also bought a pink leash and a pink harness. Dad teased Mom telling her that it wouldn't matter and no one would know if the collar was pink or blue.

Mom answered him, "But I will."

They stood in one aisle for a while debating the proper size of crate. Mom was suggesting a smaller crate; Dad, a much larger one. Mom finally gave up, and they bought the one that Dad had selected. She was sure that the crate Dad wanted was going to be too big. Because they were buying the larger crate, it meant they also needed to get a larger crate pad to fit.

Once out at the car, Dad realized that the crate that they had gotten was huge, but they decided to keep it anyway. They figured out to arrange the seats of the truck to put the crate into it safely and so that someone could reach into the crate if necessary. They then drove home and came into the house. They carried everything but the crate and crate pad inside with them. We gathered around to see what they had gotten. Duffy was interested in the treats, and I was looking at the little squeaky toys that they had gotten. Then Mom showed us the collar and harness, and it suddenly became clear—we were getting a puppy!

Mom looked at Duffy and me and told us that they were going to go on a drive to Maryland the next day to pick up a little girl puppy. Her name was Kitty, and Duffy and I both thought that was a silly name for a puppy. I especially didn't like having a puppy named Kitty because I was afraid that she would want my toy Kitty. Mom was a mind reader because she immediately reassured me that my Kitty was in a safe place and that she was going to put Duffy's lamb chop toy in the same safe place to keep it safe from the new puppy. We were both relieved that Mom knew how important those toys were to us.

True to their word, Mom and Dad left the house incredibly early the next morning, and it was pretty late in the day when they got back home. Duffy and I spent the day napping and wondering about the new puppy. Duffy wondered what made girl puppies different from boy puppies, and while I couldn't explain all of the differences, I told him a bit about my sisters Molly June and Sophie.

I told him that they were just like us and that they liked to play many of the same games. I told him how Molly June was happiest snuggling on the couch with treats. Sophie was going to dog shows, which are like beauty pageants for dogs. In short, I explained that girl dogs and boy dogs liked to play the same things, and eat the same things, and do the same things but that everyone had their own preferences.

It was late in the afternoon when we heard the truck pull up in the driveway. We both ran to the front door to meet Kitty, but we were surprised when Dad stood there alone. Where was Mom? Where was Kitty? Dad came on into the house and let both Duffy and me out to go potty in the backyard. He gave us some time to run around and smell all of the familiar smells. We also made sure to patrol the wooded part of the yard to chase any squirrels that might be there. Duffy chased a squirrel up one tree, but he did not notice when that squirrel ran down another tree and then over to the neighbor's yard.

Once we were both a little out of breath, Dad came over to us and put our leashes on. This was very unusual because we never had to wear our leashes in the yard. Duffy complained more than I did, but no one was surprised by that. I was being the proper big brother, trying to show Duffy how to act, so I sat quietly at the end of my leash. Dad then told both Duffy and me to walk over to the deck, and then he surprised us by tying our leashes to the railing.

With that, Mom came through the gate with a fluffy tiny puppy. Duffy and I both strained on our leashes to be allowed to get closer, but Dad held us back. Dad then untied my leash and walked me slowly over to where Kitty was standing. We politely sniffed each other, and she wagged her little button tail. Mom had put a few of our toys in Kitty's crate so that she could get a little familiar with our scent, so my smells were not entirely strange to her. But I think she was surprised I was so much bigger than she.

I bent down in a play bow, inviting her to play. She stood there looking at me, so I tried again. Still nothing. In fact, she seemed a bit confused by the bows, so I gave up and went back over to her and gave her a thorough sniffing. Meanwhile, she continued to twist and turn all different directions while trying to sniff me better. I decided that she was okay and gave a little wag to my tail to let Mom and Dad know that I was happy to meet Kitty.

Once Mom and Dad were comfortable with how Kitty and I were with each other, Dad went and got Duffy. Duffy was a bit rougher with his greeting and nearly knocked her over. Kitty did not appreciate that and even growled a little bit. Duffy wasn't sure how to react to this tiny puppy growling at him. I told him to relax and that she probably did not know any better. I had sensed that she may have been taken from her puppy mom too early, just like Duffy, and did not learn some of those puppy behaviors. I was confident that I could teach her those things but knew that it would take some time.

While I was thinking those things, I watched as Duffy and Kitty circled each other. She was trying desperately to sniff him, and at the same time, he was trying to sniff her. I realized that it seemed as though neither had much experience meeting other dogs, so I was glad to have been able to give a little bit of an example. I was happy that I knew how to introduce myself, but I was also just a little worried about how Kitty and Duffy would get along.

We went into the house, and Kitty instantly decided that she should have the prime spot on the couch. I wasn't too happy about it, but that really angered Duffy. Mom told Duffy to leave Kitty alone but, at the same time, put Kitty down on the floor. Kitty looked surprised by that and went over to Dad to see if he would lift her onto the couch. He reached down and gave her a pat but didn't try to move Duffy from his spot on the couch. I really didn't want to give up my spot next to Mom, but I did move enough that Kitty could be on the couch with the rest of us. That sort of worked, but Kitty would consistently try to stretch out and take over the whole couch. For such a tiny puppy, she sure could take up a lot of room!

Kitty and Duffy had gotten off on the wrong foot, and it looked like it might stay that way. Kitty felt that Duffy was being too bossy, and Duffy did not like Kitty refusing to do as he said. It took all of my energy to explain them to each other.

I reminded Duffy that he didn't always understand what other dogs were saying and that I had had to teach him how to read dog body language. He nodded slowly as he remembered. He admitted that he was still sometimes confused by dog body language, and he was thankful that I had learned to understand what they were saying. I pointed out to Kitty that Duffy was her big brother and she was the little sister and that she should listen to him. He knew a lot about being a dog in a pack and that she could learn from him.

Kitty plopped down and pouted. She announced that she didn't want to listen to anybody but Dad. She went so far as to announce that she wasn't going to take orders from anyone else. I growled at her softly, and she looked up at me with her beautiful golden eyes brimming with tears. She did not expect that growl from me! I reminded her that Duffy and I were both her big brothers and that she would listen to us. This was not a question; it was not a request. This was the order of our pack, and she needed to follow that order of things. She obviously wasn't happy with my pronouncement, but she grudgingly agreed to the rule.

I then told both Kitty and Duffy that they would both behave, they would be nice to each other, and they would not cause trouble. I was the senior dog in the household, and they would listen to me. Of course, Mom and Dad could overrule my instructions, but if they did not say anything, my bark ruled. Duffy glanced over at Kitty and quietly said that he would try to be nice. Kitty looked from me to Duffy and back to me.

She said, "I'll listen to you but not to Duffy. He's not the boss of me."

I rolled my eyes. She was going to be a handful! I reminded Kitty that she was the youngest member of our pack and that we both outranked her. She flopped down with another pout and an overly dramatic sigh. I thanked her for her agreement and walked away.

I heard her say, "I didn't agree to anything!"

I kept walking. I didn't want to argue with her.

Later Duffy thanked me for standing up to her for him. He commented that he wished he could have the same confidence that I did and that he was glad that I was his big brother. I playfully nudged him and said that he was the best little brother I could have. I told him that I would be counting on him to help teach Kitty the puppy lessons that she had missed. I knew that this would both help build Duffy's confidence and help reinforce the lessons for him.

We all learned very quickly that Kitty did not like being in her crate. She whined, cried, and barked anytime she was in there. She even tried to chew her way out of the crate. When I got a chance, I talked to her about it. I learned that I had guessed correctly—she had been taken from her dog mom too early, and she had not learned those early puppy lessons. She had not come from a huge dog farm, like Duffy, but from someone who just wanted to have some puppies. She was taken from her mom and put in a crate, where she spent most of her day. No wonder she didn't like the crate! I tried to tell her how much I liked my crate, but she just looked at me as though I was crazy.

In spite of Kitty's hatred of her crate, things settled into a new routine. We would all play together or nap together. Gradually Kitty learned to accept her crate and would willingly go in for her dinner. She still did not like sleeping in her crate and did everything she could to avoid it. I did not understand that because I really liked sleeping in my crate. I felt safe and secure in there even if the door wasn't closed.

At least once a week, Mom and Dad would put all of us in the car, and we would go for a ride. Duffy and I always enjoyed car rides, but that changed once Kitty was in the car with us. She did not like the car at all and cried nearly the entire ride. Duffy and I tried to convince her that car rides were good, but she did not agree. We learned from talking with her that, before she came to live with us, car rides were always to see the doctor; and her doctor in Maryland was not nice. Kitty liked Dr. Barbara, our doctor, but she was still learning to trust everyone else.

Mom and Dad made a point of stopping by the local ice-cream shop nearly every car ride. They wanted to help Kitty think of something good when she thought of car rides. Duffy and I didn't complain; we loved getting our little cups of peanut butter vanilla ice cream! Gradually Kitty learned that car rides were typically good things and that she didn't need to be so afraid all of the time. That didn't mean that she stopped crying in the car. She told me once that she was afraid that, if she stopped crying in the car, Mom and Dad wouldn't get us ice cream any longer. As much as I tried to convince her that the ice cream would still happen, she still cried while riding in the car. Sisters can be so frustrating.

One time, Kitty went for a car ride without me or Duffy. That ride was to visit a special friend of Mom and Dad. Toni was a breeder who loved wheaten terriers. I met Toni once or twice, and I thought she was really nice just like my breeder, Cam.

Both Toni and Cam are considered good breeders, taking their time with the puppies and making sure that they have enough time with their mom dogs to learn the important puppy lessons. They also introduce their puppies to lots of new experiences so that, when they go to their forever homes, they are happy and well-adjusted pups.

There are lots of not-so-good breeders, like the one who owned Duffy's mom. Duffy was taken from his mom dog far too soon, and he hadn't learned all of his puppy lessons. We all assumed the same was true with Kitty, especially since her tail was so short. You see, wheaten terriers often have shortened tails because of the traditions from Ireland where our breed got started. That's changing now, but both Duffy and I had tails that were about five inches long. A natural or undocked tail is about twelve inches long. Anyway, Kitty's tail was barely an inch long, just a little button of a tail.

Toni lived a few towns away from our house and offered to give Kitty her first grooming. Mom said that it was amazing to watch Kitty transform from a fluffy dog-shaped animal into a beautiful young wheaten-terrier lady. Kitty behaved perfectly for Toni and then had a little playtime with Toni's pup, Luba. Kitty and Luba were sad when it was time for Kitty to go home, but Mom and Toni promised them another playdate sometime in the future. I will admit that I almost did not recognize Kitty when she got home; she was just that beautiful. Kitty was a bit shy when Duffy exclaimed how pretty she was and almost ran to hide when I echoed his comments. She wasn't used to getting praise.

When Mom and Dad got home with Kitty, Mom announced that she wanted to get a few pictures of Kitty after her haircut. Mom dug through one of the drawers in her bedroom and came back holding a tiny bow. She carefully clipped the bow into Kitty's hair and stepped back to take a photograph. It is incredibly good that she was able to take the picture quickly because Kitty was almost as fast as she reached up with her paw to sweep the bow from her head. It became a battle of wills as Mom put the bow back in Kitty's hair for another picture and Kitty fought to keep it off. I never told Kitty, but I thought she looked really cute with the tiny bow in her hair.

One evening, after Kitty had lived with us for about two months, Mom came out of her office extremely excited.

"She's ours!" she announced.

Kitty was officially adopted, and she was now part of our family forever. Dad got up from his chair and hugged Kitty.

While hugging her, he whispered to her, "You are now our little girl forever, and we are changing your name to erase your old life."

Suddenly Kitty was being called Ciara. I personally thought that her new name was much prettier. It took everyone a few days to get used to calling her Ciara, but it was soon hard to remember her old name. Kitty, oops, Ciara seemed to like her new name and confided to me that she was especially relieved when she learned that she would never have to leave our family.

Over time, our individual personality traits became obvious. Of course, I had always been the thinker. I was content to sit and watch the world, soaking up sun puddles and taking life easily. Dad called Duffy a linebacker. He was sturdy and solid and ran into life full speed. If anyone heard a crash, it was almost certainly the result of Duffy running into something. Ciara chose to take things a little more slowly but was always ready for a rough-and-tumble game of chase with Duffy. Her preferred spot, however, was on the couch next to Dad. It hadn't taken long for her to wrap him around her paw, and she only had to look at him to get belly rubs or treats. She was the family diva.

For most of the time, Duffy and Ciara got along best when we were outside. I still liked to sit at the fence and watch the people and cars, and Duffy and Ciara would chase the squirrels. Duffy liked chasing after balls that either Mom or Dad would throw, but Ciara would not give a ball a second look. Just like my other puppy brothers and sisters, we three had our own personalities.

Ciara grew into being an incredibly good hunter. She would chase after the chipmunks and squirrels. She almost caught them a few times! Duffy would chase them too, but they seemed to always outsmart him and go up a different tree than he expected. Ciara would laugh at him, and that would make Duffy mad.

"Sisters!" he would grumble to me.

Duffy liked to jump up onto the furniture outside, and each time he did it, Mom would laugh and call him circus dog. He really enjoyed walking the bench around one of the trees. I think he was pretending that he was in the Olympics or something.

Ciara would get herself into trouble very often because she liked to dig. One day, she had to run away from her newly dug hole very quickly because a chair toppled into it. Dad was not happy with her for that, but she snuggled next to him and wagged her little tail. He looked into her brown eyes and couldn't stay mad at her. Mom and Dad were always looking for ways to discourage Ciara from digging, but most of their ideas failed.

Ciara still hated to ride in the car, but fortunately that didn't stop Mom and Dad from continuing to take us on hikes. Dad and Mom had gotten Ciara her own pack, and we all hiked together. Mom usually clipped Ciara's pack and my pack together and held our leash while Dad held Duffy's leash by himself. This arrangement worked well because Ciara and Duffy couldn't bicker the entire hike. I didn't mind being together with Ciara although she nearly pulled me off of my feet a time or two when she started to chase after some little rodent. I think she resented that I kept her from being able to run after them. We all enjoyed our hiking adventures, and I was really happy that we kept the tradition of stopping for ice cream on the way home. Peanut butter vanilla was always my favorite!

We spent most evenings at home, and we all enjoyed that special time together. We had all decided on our favorite spots for cuddle time, and you could find us in our places most evenings. I preferred to snuggle on the couch with Mom. Ciara was on the other end of the couch with Dad. Duffy liked sleeping on feet, so he would pick either Mom's feet or Dad's feet to use as a pillow while we all relaxed in the TV room.

When bedtime came, I took my rightful spot on the big bed between Mom and Dad. Ciara lay at Dad's feet, and Duffy curled up in the hallway. Mom and Dad kept a small light on in the hallway because they had figured out that Duffy did not like the dark. It never bothered me, but I was really impressed that they had been able to help Duffy simply by leaving a light on for him. They were good dog parents. Looking back on it, life was incredibly good.

Mom's Hurt

One afternoon, after we came in from playing in the yard, I wandered down the hallway toward the TV room; and Dad was setting up the gate again. When we were puppies, Mom and Dad had a gate across the hallway to keep us close to them. I didn't realize, when they put the gate in the hallway before Duffy came to live with us, exactly what it meant; but I understood the meaning of the gate when they brought Ciara home.

What had me a bit confused this time, though, was the placement of the gate. Dad was using it to close off the guest bedroom. We almost never used that room although I did like to nap on the bed in there. Ciara and Duffy never thought to look for me there. The sun came in through that window, and a sun puddle nearly always formed at the center of that bed—my most favorite nap spot.

Anyway, I couldn't figure out what Dad was doing. I watched as he carried one of the dining room chairs into that room, along with a folding table. He carefully put sheets and lots of pillows onto the bed, along with a large tray holding some pens and pencils and a couple of books. This was extremely perplexing.

Later that evening, when Mom came home from work, Dad proudly showed here what he had done. She looked approvingly at what he had done and said that he had done an excellent job. She looked a bit worried and then went to gather a few more things to put on the tray. Once she was done, she closed the gate. She turned and saw me sitting in the hall, so I tilted my head to let her know that I had a few questions.

She came over to me and bent down. She gave me a hug and said that she was going to go away for a few days so that her doctor could fix her knee. They were setting up the guest room for her to use once she got back from the people hospital.

She went on to remind me that, when I came home from the hospital after I cut my back, I spent a lot of my time in my crate so that Duffy couldn't bump me or hurt me. I thought hard and remembered that, so I guessed that they were making the guest room into a people-sized crate for Mom. I wondered then if she would have to wear a cone to keep from bothering her knee. I started to get the giggles thinking about Mom wearing a cone, but since that was undignified, I gave a little bark instead.

A few days later, Mom and Dad got up early in the morning, even earlier than they did when they had to go to work. Once they were dressed, we went outside, and I was surprised to discover that it had snowed overnight. We had great fun slipping and sliding through the snow, but Dad cut our fun short and made us come in.

As we trudged into the house from our morning potty and playtime, I saw that Mom had a small knapsack with her. It looked like the one she used when she traveled, so I guessed this was the day that she was going to go to the people hospital. I saw her put a few things into the bag, but it didn't really seem like it was enough stuff if she was going to be away for a few days. She gave the bag to Dad and asked him to keep track of it until she was ready for it after surgery.

When I heard her say surgery, I got extra worried. I remembered how groggy I felt after my surgery way back when I cut my back and that I had to stay at the hospital for a few days until they were satisfied that I was getting better. That meant that Mom wouldn't be home again for a few days. I woofed my concerns, startling everyone. Mom came over to me and rubbed my ears. She thanked me for being worried but said that she was confident everything would be okay. She then looked at Duffy and Ciara and told them that they had to listen to Dad and me while she was away. I don't think Duffy minded those instructions, but I know Ciara was a bit hurt that Mom didn't put her in charge.

With that, they made their way out of the house and to the truck. I jumped up on the couch and watched out the window until

I couldn't see the truck's taillights any longer. I suddenly felt very alone and worried.

I then decided that time would pass more quickly with a nap, but that was easier said than done. Ciara wanted to know where Mom and Dad were going, how long they would be gone, what would be happening, and on and on. I had to admit to her that I didn't know the answers to most of her questions but that I was sure that Dad would be taking good care of Mom while they were gone.

We were all surprised when the door opened around lunchtime and our favorite dog sitter came in the front door. Vicki was as happy to see us as we were to see her, and after giving her a good and proper wheaten greeting, we went outside to potty and play. I know I was disappointed to discover that the snow had mostly melted, but there were still a few patches here and there that I could roll in and feel that wonderful coldness.

After a nice playtime outside, Vicki invited us inside for some treats. When we got back inside, she gave us each one of our favorite chewy treats. While we were outside, Vicki had picked up the pillows that Ciara had pushed off of the couch, and she refilled our water bowls.

As Vicki got ready to leave again, I hopped up onto the couch to resume my nap. There wasn't much sun, but there was a cozy blanket to snuggle with. My favorite afternoon napping spot was behind the gate in the guest room, so this would have to do. I was asleep almost before Vicki left. All of that cold air and playtime made me sleepy.

The next time the door opened, it was dark outside. I almost expected to see Vicki again, but this time, it was Dad. I jumped up to look behind him to see if Mom was coming up the front steps, but he was alone. I sat down and looked at him, tilting my head to ask where Mom was.

Dad reached down and rubbed my ears a bit and said, "Mom has to stay overnight so that they can make sure her knee works properly."

That didn't really make sense. Why wouldn't her knee work? But I didn't bother Dad anymore. He looked really tired, and it did not take long for him to fall asleep once he sat on the couch in the

TV room. His nap didn't last for more than a few minutes because Ciara started crying and barking for her dinner.

Dad got up, grumbling a bit, and fixed our dinners. He then stood at the door and watched as we made our after-dinner potty trip out back. Once we were all back inside, Dad opened a bag of chips, poured some into a bowl, and settled back into his place on the couch. He put on one of his favorite TV shows and was snoring loudly within a few minutes. He had left his bowl on the little table next to him, and Ciara was quietly sneaking chips from the bowl. She did share, dropping a few to the floor for Duffy and me to enjoy. Everything was working well for us until Ciara got greedy and knocked the bowl to the floor. That noise woke Dad up, and while he did scoop up most of the chips, both Duffy and I were each able to grab a decent mouthful before he got everything picked up.

Sometime later, Dad got up and went to bed. Naturally, Ciara hopped up onto the bed next to him, and she claimed Mom's spot. I wasn't too happy about that, so I jumped up and made myself comfortable on Mom's side of the bed, happily resting my head on her pillow. I went to sleep enjoying Mom's scent from her pillow.

The next day felt really strange. Dad was home, but Mom wasn't. I know that is exactly the same as when Dad stays home and Mom goes to work, but this felt different. I knew she wasn't at work and she wasn't home. She was still at the hospital, learning how to use her new knee, from what Dad said.

Later that afternoon, Dad left the house. He explained that he was going to see Mom and he would tell her how much we missed her. He took a couple of books with him, mumbling that he hoped he had grabbed the right ones.

I guess that they were because, when Dad came home, he had different books with him. Dad put those on the table in the living room, right next to another stack of books. I wondered why there were two stacks but decided that people sometimes do unusual things without explanation.

The next morning, Dad moved the taller stack of books into the guest room and put them on the floor next to the bed. I wondered what that meant, but I could tell that Dad wasn't in the mood to answer any questions. He was rushing around putting dishes in the dishwasher and picking up sweaters from the living room, all very curious behavior.

Again, later in the afternoon, Dad left. This time, he remembered to tell us to be good while he was away. That was an easy assignment for me, I thought, as I hopped up onto the couch for a nap.

Sometime later, we heard the truck pull into the driveway. Dad came in and immediately took us out back so that we could potty. This wasn't anything unusual, but it felt as though he had an extra urgency in wanting us to go outside, do our business, and come back inside.

I guess I was right because it wasn't very long before he called for us to come inside. We all ran to the door for two reasons. First it was cold outside, and second Dad was holding some of our favorite chewy treats. We all sat like we were taught in our puppy classes, took our treats gently, then started into the main part of the house to enjoy them.

Suddenly I stopped. I knew Mom was home. I could smell her! Still holding my treat, I raced down the hall into the TV room and was disappointed to realize that she wasn't there. I then ran to the bedroom. No Mom. Surely my nose wasn't failing me! Then I remembered the guest room.

I whirled around and ran to the gate. There on the bed with pillows all around her lay Mom. I was so happy to see her. I sat at the gate and woofed softly. I didn't want to startle her.

She looked over toward the door, where I sat properly behind the gate, and said, "Hi, Quincy. I've missed you."

I whined a little because I couldn't get through the gate to snuggle with Mom.

Dad came up behind me and rubbed my ears. "Maybe after Mom has a little rest, I can let you in, Quincy. I know you'll be gentle."

By then, Duffy and Ciara had realized that Mom was home, and they came racing down the hall, nearly knocking me off of my feet. Duffy jumped up and put his paws on the top of the gate, and

Dad told him to get down. Ciara simply sat and whined. We were each telling Mom in our own ways that we had missed her.

Mom reached down and picked up one of the books from the stack Dad had relocated earlier in the day. She smiled and said, "I'm going to read for a little while, at least until I fall asleep."

I curled up by the gate, and I honestly don't think that she read more than a page or two before I heard her softly snoring.

Later that evening, Dad opened the gate and let me in to snuggle next to Mom. She showed me exactly where I could be so that I didn't hurt her sore leg. I was so happy to be able to be with her! Dad brought her dinner to her, and Mom suggested that he bring mine to me as well. Dad chuckled but did as she asked.

Duffy and Ciara were a little annoyed that I was getting preferential treatment, but I quietly reminded Duffy that Mom and I had a special relationship. She called me her heart dog. I filled up special places in her heart that no one else could.

I did my best to cuddle Mom as much as I could over the next couple of weeks while she recovered. I was lucky because she let me be in the little room with her, and I know that Ciara and Duffy were disappointed that Mom didn't give them the same privileges.

I did have to leave the room when Mom had her physical therapy. I could tell that the therapists did not impress her, but she did take their papers with the exercises and diligently did them in between their visits. I know she was happy when the visiting therapists gave her the go-ahead to start regular physical therapy at what she called the real therapy place. That was where she went for physical therapy when she hurt her shoulder, and she really liked her therapist there.

We were all excited when her therapist gave her a set of homework exercises that included the directive to go walking. We knew that did not mean hiking, but Mom would take my leash in one hand and her cane in the other. We would slowly walk through the neighborhood. It did not seem to be very long before Mom gave up the cane, and we just walked carefully, avoiding those little rocks and things that could have made her fall.

I was proud of my mom when she came home from therapy one day and said that she had been discharged from therapy and her knee was doing exceptionally well.

She then came over to me and gave me a great big hug, saying, "And I know it was my private nurse and therapist, Quincy, who speeded my recovery along."

Duffy's Sick

When Ciara first came to live with us, she and Duffy would fight a little. I think they were both just trying to figure out which one of them was the boss. Ciara felt that she should be in charge because she was Dad's favorite little girl, and Duffy thought he should be in charge because he had lived with Mom and Dad longer than Ciara. They never fought with me. They knew that I was the most senior wheaten in the house, so they had to listen to me.

As time went on, I didn't have to be a referee for their fights. They gradually learned to tolerate each other and would even play together, especially if we were outside. In fact, Dad would say that they had to hold each other's paws to go outside together. They would play endless games of chase while I preferred to sit in one of the deck chairs and watch them run themselves silly.

We all had our favorite places to relax inside the house, and they varied depending on the time of day. During the daytime, I liked to lie on the couch in the living room. The sun would come in through the window at certain times during the morning, and I loved lying in that warmth. Duffy spent his mornings on the chair on the other side of the room, and Ciara would take her spot on the floor at Dad's feet. Dad didn't have to go to work, and that made Ciara very happy. We all had our places in the TV room in the evenings, and mine was right next to Mom.

Everything moved along quite smoothly for a few years, but over time, I noticed that Duffy was gradually getting grumpier. He was almost ten years old when I first noticed it, and I'd asked him a number of times if there was something wrong. He assured me that he was fine; but I also suspect that, if there was something wrong, he wouldn't admit it to anyone. I think that he was afraid that, if Ciara learned he was sick, she would try harder to become the boss of him. Still I worried about him.

One day in mid-autumn, Mom was quite excited by something good that had happened for her at work. To celebrate, Mom and Dad invited one of their friends to join them for a celebration dinner. Duffy, Ciara, and I were excited because I overheard them saying that they were going to go to a special restaurant for steaks. I knew that there would be leftovers that they would share with us so that we could celebrate with them. We didn't get leftovers very often, so this was something to really look forward to enjoying.

When Mom, Dad, and their friend Barbara left our house, everything seemed normal. Duffy and Ciara were avoiding one another, and I was on the couch keeping an eye on them. Even though I didn't move so fast anymore and I was getting old, they would still listen to me.

Duffy started to pace, and he said that he didn't feel well. He felt like he wanted to throw up, but he couldn't. He had a tough time getting comfortable and was really quite grumpy. I told Ciara to go over to the couch while I talked privately with Duffy. She didn't want to at first. She whined a bit, but I growled at her. She scooted over to the couch. I didn't growl often, but when I did, everyone knew that there was no point in continuing to argue. I gently nudged Duffy to join me in the dining room to talk, and that was when he admitted that he hadn't been feeling well for a while. He also said that he felt worse right then than he ever had before. We talked a little bit more, and then both Ciara and I stayed well out of his way as he struggled to find a position that felt good.

Duffy was stretched out on the floor when Mom, Dad, and their friend Barbara came in.

Dad looked at Duffy and announced, "Something's wrong!"

Mom bent down and lifted Duffy's lip. She later said that she expected to see normal pink gums or bright-red gums indicating that he had an infection. When his gums were a very pale gray, she jumped up and called the emergency vet.

Mom described what was going on, and it did not take very long at all for the decision to come that they needed to bring Duffy to the dog emergency room. Mom paused a moment to make another quick phone call to leave a message for Dr. Barbara's office to let them know that Duffy was on his way to the emergency vet and that his gums were extremely pale. This is one of the easiest ways to tell if a dog is sick, and Mom was glad that she had thought to check.

Meanwhile, their friend Barbara had gathered Mom and Dad's leftover steak and put it into the refrigerator. She said that she wanted to be useful, and that was the only thing that she could think of to do. She then left to go to her house but asked that Mom keep her up to date with what was going on. Mom promised that she would call later to give an update.

Dad carried Duffy out to the car and gently placed him in the back. Duffy was making really sad noises, and it was truly upsetting to everyone. Looking back on it now, when they left, both Ciara and I cried loudly too. I think we had realized how sick Duffy was, and we were letting him know that we were quite worried about him. It wasn't something that we planned, but we both cried loudly as they left.

I wasn't there; but I later learned what happened after Mom, Dad, and Duffy left. As they were driving to the emergency veterinarian, Duffy was whimpering and crying. He really did not feel well and was hurting very badly. When they got to the hospital, he walked in slowly between Mom and Dad. He was hoping that they could help him feel better.

The technicians lifted him onto a rolling stretcher and carefully removed his collar and leash and handed them to Mom. They said that they didn't want to risk losing it in the back. Dad took the leash from Mom and cradled it in his hands. They started to move toward the waiting room when one of the technicians suggested that they sit in an empty exam room to wait.

Mom and Dad sat in that tiny room wordlessly mulling over the possibilities.

Mom finally looked at Dad and said quietly, "He won't be going home with us."

Dad silently nodded. Mom reached into her pocket and pulled out her phone. She texted her friend Sherry, remembering that Sherry had experienced something terribly similar with her Bailey only a few short months before. Sherry texted back that she shared Mom's concern and would be thinking about everyone.

After a while, a veterinarian came into the room where Mom and Dad were waiting. He explained that they had taken an x-ray and did not like what they saw.

He started to say what his thoughts were when Mom interrupted and said, "Ruptured tumor."

The doctor was quite surprised and stuttered a bit as he asked, "Yes, that's what we think, and how did you know?"

Mom sighed and said that the timeline matched what her friend had experienced and that was why she wasn't surprised by what he had said. The veterinarian started to offer some suggestions.

Dad interrupted him. "We promised that we would not be selfish and do anything for us that didn't make Duffy's life better."

With that, they explained that they did not want Duffy to have to have surgery when there would be no promise of a long life afterward. The doctor nodded and said that he would get everything ready for Duffy's trip to the Rainbow Bridge.

Before I go on, let me explain a little bit about the Rainbow Bridge. That's a special place in heaven where dogs wait for their humans to come meet them before going all of the way into the main part of heaven. The dogs at the Rainbow Bridge can communicate with their people here on earth by leaving white feathers when they visit. The Rainbow Bridge pups visit when their people are upset or when they need just a bit of special comfort. The dog visitors leave white feathers for their people to find so that they know about the visit and that we all still love each other.

A little while later, the veterinarian came and walked with Mom and Dad as they went into another room. This room was off to the side of the main hallway and was set up with a couple of couches, soft lighting, and some gentle music. Dad sat on the couch while Mom sat on one of the comfortable chairs.

After a few minutes, the technician brought Duffy into the room. He was resting on a low rolling bed and had a couple of blankets tucked around him. The technician explained that they had given Duffy some medicine to make him feel a little better, but it was also making him sleepy.

Mom slid onto the floor and rested her nose up against Duffy's as she rubbed his ears. She and Dad told Duffy what a brave and good boy he was and that they would miss him very much. Mom told him to go looking for Bailey when he got to the Rainbow Bridge because he had been there for a few months and would be a good friend for Duffy.

Duffy watched Mom with his beautiful brown eyes, but she could tell that he really wanted to rest. She kissed his nose and let the technician know that it was time for Duffy to make his final journey. The technician came and gave Duffy some more medicine. As Duffy went to sleep, he could feel Mom and Dad giving him pets, rubs, and kisses.

They gave him one last hug and quietly slipped out of the side door. They carried his collar and the leash and a small bag with a little of his hair. Once out at the car, Mom sent a message to Bailey's mom, Sherry, to tell her that Duffy was on his way to meet Bailey. They sat in the car for a little while, trying to understand how things had changed so quickly. Mom also let their friend Barbara know that Duffy had died.

After a quiet drive home, Mom and Dad came into the house. Ciara and I greeted them gently. We knew that they had just said goodbye to Duffy and that they were incredibly sad. We didn't jump or bark but leaned in quietly instead. We wanted them to know that we were sad too.

I went and sat with Mom, with my head resting on her knee. She was staring off into space with a faraway look in her eyes. Her hand gently rubbed my ears, but I know she was thinking about Duffy. Ciara and I probably understood better than they did how sick he had been, and that was why he had been so grumpy lately. I hoped that they didn't think about that, though, because I didn't want them to feel any worse than they already did.

Ciara was sitting at Dad's feet, leaning into his legs. She whined a bit to try to remind him that we hadn't had our dinner yet, but he wasn't listening to her.

She finally stood up and put her paw into the dinner dish and told him, "Woof!"

He looked startled and then realized that she wanted to eat. He got up and went to the kitchen to get our dinners ready.

Mom went into the office, intending to sit at her computer to write a message to all of our friends. She wanted to let them know about Duffy and to ask them to hug their wheaten just a bit tighter. She first reached up on the shelf to put his collar there so that it would be safe until she could put it into a memory box. As she turned to her desk, a small white feather floated onto her keyboard. She picked it up and looked at it in amazement. There was absolutely no good reason for a feather to have been on that shelf. She then remembered that pups at the Rainbow Bridge use feathers to let their people know that they are safe. She put the feather with Duffy's collar that she would later add to his memory box.

Without Duffy, the house felt really quiet—too quiet. Ciara snuggled with Dad while I leaned against Mom. I felt badly that Mom had to go to work the day after Duffy died because I knew that she really needed lots of extra cuddles, and I couldn't be there for her. I made sure that I was with her as much as I could be when she was home.

Ciara was really upset. She curled up next to me and whimpered softly that she didn't mean to be unkind to Duffy. She felt bad for fighting with him. She asked me if I thought that Duffy knew just how much everyone loved him. I assured her that he did, and then we shared stories about our time with Duffy. I knew most of the stories that Ciara told me about her time with Duffy, but it was interesting to hear her view. She told me that she liked going outside with Duffy because he would always look around to make sure that there were no big dogs around. I hadn't known that Ciara was afraid of big dogs, but Duffy knew that. I promised her that I would protect her from big dogs if she would protect me from little dogs.

She smiled a little and said, "Of course."

We both laughed a little because no other dogs could get into our backyard.

Ciara pressed me to tell her stories about Duffy before she came to live with us. I told her about our trip to the beach and how much we enjoyed hiking. When I told her about the long car rides to go on those vacations, she shook her head. She did not like riding in the car even if it meant a good hike or a cup of ice cream.

Bedtime that night was really hard. Duffy and I would often lie in the TV room after everyone else had gone to bed and talk. We really were best of friends. I didn't want to be in the TV room by myself, but I also didn't want to be on the bed with Ciara since she didn't make it easy for me to lie next to Mom.

Mom must have been thinking the same thing because she came into the TV room and settled into her spot on the couch. She pulled a blanket over her legs and shifted her seat into the recline position. She then patted the couch next to her, and I didn't hesitate at all. I jumped up and curled up next to her. I fell asleep with her hand resting gently on my back. I know that comforted me, and I think I helped to make her feel better too.

It took a little while, but after a few days, we all settled into a new routine. It felt strange not having Duffy around to talk to, and I know that everyone else was missing him. The house felt empty without him clomping through the house, and I missed hearing him bark at the delivery trucks. I hoped that he was free from pain and having a fun time at the Rainbow Bridge. That night, he surprised me with a feather on my bed. That made me feel a bit better, but I still wished he was here with us.

Welcome, Alvin!

Mom and Dad talked about getting another pup, but they were both really sad. Everyone was missing Duffy. Duffy got sick and went to the Rainbow Bridge very quickly, so they were trying to get accustomed to Duffy not being with us. Mom said something about not wanting to add another pup because of my age, thinking that it would not be fair to me. Dad thought that a puppy might help me stay more active. I wasn't sure what I thought about either idea but figured they would know what was best.

Ciara and I talked about it a little bit too. She definitely didn't want a little sister. She was afraid that another girl might break up the special bond that she had with Daddy. She wasn't convinced that a little brother would be a good thing either because of the way that she and Duffy sometimes fought. I reminded her that, if Mom and Dad brought a puppy home, that puppy would be younger than her; so she'd be a big sister. That sort of convinced her that it might be okay, but she really wasn't entirely sure.

I didn't know either. I'd been the big brother when Duffy came to our house and then the bigger brother when Ciara came to our family. Duffy and I were best buddies, so that worked out okay. But Ciara had been a bit demanding and a bit of a princess. I wasn't sure if I could handle another princess either.

One evening, about three weeks after Duffy died, Ciara and I were napping on the floor of the TV room. Mom was typing on her computer tablet, and she handed her tablet over to Dad and told him to read something. I rolled over so that I could watch Dad's face as he read whatever it was that Mom wanted him to read. I could learn a lot about what was going on just by watching their expressions. This time, their faces didn't tell me much, and I guessed I was going to have to wait to learn what was going on.

Dad handed the tablet back to Mom and said, "Well, what do you want to do?"

She sighed heavily and said, "I really don't know."

I could tell that their conversation was going to take a while, so I rolled back over to take another nap. Well, that was my plan until Ciara put her paw on my head and leaned down.

"What do you think they're talking about?" she asked.

I decided that it would be easier to talk to Ciara in the other room; so I got up, stretched, and walked down the hall to the kitchen for a drink of water. She followed me, not realizing that I was stalling for time!

I could hear snippets of the conversation between Mom and Dad.

"He's only twenty-one weeks old."

"Irish coat."

"Oh, look at this picture!"

"What should be his name?"

By the time I heard that last question, I'd figured out that Ciara and I were going to have a new baby brother.

"Um, Ciara, I think you're going to have a little brother," I said.

"What? *When?* How?" she barked.

I explained what I'd overheard and told her to relax. She then started to whine that she didn't want a new puppy to get her favorite toys, or her bed, or her place next to Dad. She continued to list what she didn't want the puppy to have while I left her in the living room and walked back to the TV room. I couldn't listen to her anymore.

Mom was on the phone as I came into the room, and I listened as she was confirming that we would gladly welcome "the blue puppy" into our home. I knew that he was called the blue puppy because that was the color of his very first puppy collar. Mom and Dad would give him a proper name.

About a week later, Mom and Dad gathered all sorts of puppy things together, just as they did when they went to get Ciara. I watched as they put my exercise pen into the car, along with the bag of treats, water, bowls, and a collar. Instead of going out to get a new crate, though, they put Duffy's crate in the truck to take with them. That made me just a little sad because I knew that the new puppy smells would cover up Duffy's smells, but we still had some of Duffy's toys around that I could sniff to remember him. I had even hidden one of his toys under my bed so that Ciara couldn't get to it that I sometimes cuddled with late at night when I was really missing him.

Anyway, early the next morning, Mom and Dad left Ciara and me at the house. Dad told us to behave; and then Mom said that, when they came home later that day, they would have a little brother puppy with them. With that, they hopped into the truck and drove away. Ciara and I stood on the couch and watched them drive away. We were both filled with questions, but neither of us had answers. I decided that the couch would make a cozy nap spot, especially since I could see that the sky was gray, and it looked as though it was going to snow. Ciara hopped up and curled into a ball in Dad's chair.

Meanwhile, Mom and Dad were traveling along the highways talking about all sorts of things. Mom noticed that there were a lot of trucks on the road, so she started counting them. Dad laughed at her, teasing her a bit that she was always counting things.

Mom shrugged and said, "That's what I do."

When they got home later that evening, she made a point of telling Dad that they had seen a total of twenty-one of the brown trucks that day.

After driving for several hours, they stopped for a quick lunch. Once back on the road, they started to travel over a mountain, and the road conditions worsened. It wasn't icy yet; but Dad was a little concerned that, if their trip back home was delayed for any length of time, the roads could become slick.

They drove on for about another hour over the mountain, then pulled off of the highway and into a restaurant parking lot. The weather was much clearer down in the valley, and they parked in the far corner of the parking lot. After a brief wait, another vehicle pulled in and parked next to their truck. A man got out of the new vehicle, and Mom and Dad chatted with him for a little bit. Dad set up the exercise pen, and the new man carefully lifted a little puppy from the crate in his truck and set him down onto the grass.

The people chatted for a few minutes. The puppy pottied, and then Mom picked up the little boy puppy and gently placed him into the crate in our truck. Mom offered him a treat. The boy puppy took the goodie and chewed on it thoughtfully. I'm sure he wondered what was going on.

Mom closed the door of the crate and said to Dad that they should get started back over the mountain. They said goodbye to the other man and headed toward home. The gentle movement of the truck lulled the puppy, and soon he was snoring soft puppy snores.

Mom and Dad were relieved once they'd driven over the mountain and were back on dry roads again. The snow and ice were only in the higher parts of the mountain. They drove to the next exit after the mountain to make a quick stop. Once again, they parked, and Dad set up the exercise pen. The puppy was excited to walk around a bit inside the pen and to sniff the new and unfamiliar smells. Mom walked over to the building and got something for herself and Dad to eat while Dad put the puppy back into the crate and gave him a small bowl of food. After everyone had their snacks, Dad gave the puppy a few minutes in the exercise pen for another potty break, and then they were back on the road to home.

When Mom and Dad got home, the first thing that they did was to set up the exercise pen again, this time in our front yard. They gave the puppy a few minutes to potty and to sniff the area. While Dad watched the puppy, Mom came inside and attached my leash. Ciara looked a little confused, and I woofed softly that we were going to meet the puppy one at a time so that he didn't get overwhelmed. She nodded that she understood but still whined because she knew Dad was outside and she wanted to be with him.

I walked nicely on my leash over to the exercise pen. I wanted to show my new little brother how to behave as Dad brought me out on my leash. We sniffed each other politely through the bars of the pen, then Dad opened the gate and let me in to officially meet my new brother. Dad told me that the puppy's name was Alvin. Alvin didn't look like Duffy did when he was a puppy. Duffy was kind of round and short. Alvin had really long legs and was fairly slim. He was still a wheaten terrier puppy, but just he looked a bit different.

Once Dad was satisfied that we were getting along, he left us in the pen, with Mom supervising, and went inside to get Ciara. I could hear her excited squeals when Dad went into the house and explained to Alvin that Ciara was "Daddy's little girl." He said that one of his sisters was their human daddy's favorite little girl, so he understood.

Dad and Ciara came outside, and while Alvin and Ciara were sniffing each other through the bars of the exercise pen, Mom snapped my leash onto my collar and led me out of the pen. Once I had moved away a little bit, Dad led Ciara into the pen, and Alvin and Ciara sniffed each other all over. Alvin jumped up a bit to bite at Ciara's beard, and Ciara put her foot onto him and held him down.

"It isn't polite to annoy your sister," she woofed.

Alvin simply wagged his tail. I could see that he was going to keep us all busy.

The rest of their introduction went smoothly. After a few minutes, Dad clipped the leash back onto Ciara's collar, and Mom picked up Alvin. Once inside, Dad took off Ciara's leash and went back out to bring in the exercise pen and the bag of things that they had taken with them. Meanwhile, Ciara ran through the house as if to show Alvin that it was *her* house. I just sat next to Alvin and woofed softly that it was sometimes easier to let her think that she knew everything.

Once Dad was back inside, we settled into our favorite places in the TV room. Alvin didn't have his own special place yet, so Mom and Dad took turns holding him on their laps. He was full of energy, though, and wanted to climb up to lick their ears, then climb down to sniff their feet. Mom finally put the gate across the hallway and gently put him on the floor. He was confined to the hallway since all of the doors to the other rooms were closed, and she could see him to make sure he wasn't doing anything that he shouldn't be doing.

I wandered out into the hallway to see what Alvin was doing. He was walking around with one of Ciara's toys and sniffing the different smells in the area. I decided to lie down, and once I'd flopped down on my side, Alvin was instantly climbing on me. He tugged my ears, chewed on one of my feet a little bit, then tried to lick my nose. I woofed gently at him, and he sat down and looked at me. I then explained to him that I was senior dog and that my rules were the rules. Mom and Dad could overrule me, but unless they said something, I was in charge. Alvin nodded to show that he understood. I then told him that Ciara could be a bit bossy but that she was also interested in making sure that he grew up to be a good dog. Ciara overheard me tell him that, and she came out into the hall.

"I can be a bit bossy?" she growled.

I ignored her and told Alvin that Ciara was next in command after me. Ciara started to say something about being Dad's favorite and more in charge than me, but I gave her a dirty look. She stopped barking.

We then asked Alvin about where he had come from. He explained that he was one of nine puppies. They were born on a farm in Michigan to a particularly good breeder of champion wheaten terrier puppies. His litter had dog parents that had come from Ireland, where our breed originated, so his hair was a bit different from mine and vastly different from Ciara's. Ciara's coat was downy soft and fluffy and considered an American coat, and Alvin's hair was a bit rougher. Eventually, though, his coat will become soft and silky. My hair was closer in texture to Alvin's but still had some characteristics similar to Ciara's.

We also noticed that Alvin's tail was different. I knew that my tail had been "docked" when I was just a few days old, and it was only about five inches long. This had been the tradition for wheaten terriers until very recently. I didn't remember when they shortened my tail; I just remembered it always being short. And speaking of short, Ciara has just a nub of a tail. Mom and Dad said that was more proof that she didn't come from a good and knowledgeable wheaten breeder. Like me, she doesn't remember the day the vet cut her tail short. Alvin's tail, on the other hand, was long and arched gracefully over his back. When he wagged his tail, the fluff at the end looked a bit like a flag. I don't like to admit it, but I was just a little bit jealous of his long tail.

Alvin went on to say that, because he had lived on a farm, he enjoyed hunting things. He had been given a chance to try barn hunting, just like my brother Murphy did before we left Cam's house. Alvin had really enjoyed it and had learned some of the tricks from one of the older wheatens at his original home. That dog had won many trophies and ribbons at barn hunting, so Alvin hoped that he would get the chance to show off his skills. Ciara told him that we had mice and chipmunks in the backyard and that they were fun to chase. Alvin was excited to hear that.

The next day, Mom and Dad took Alvin to see Dr. Barbara to make sure that he was in good health and so that she could meet him when he wasn't sick. Everyone in her office made a bit of a fuss over him, and his long tail was quite the topic of conversation. Alvin behaved very well for the doctor, and I was happy to hear that.

Once Alvin saw Dr. Barbara and got the last of his puppy vaccinations, Mom and Dad started taking Alvin with us on our adventures. They got him a new backpack, and Ciara and I taught him how to hike with us. This time, Mom clipped Alvin and Ciara together, leaving me to walk by myself. I like this arrangement since I could walk a bit more slowly and not cross from side to side on the path the way that they wanted to. I enjoyed watching them, but it made me tired. I longed for some of that extra energy.

Alvin loved car rides, just like Duffy and I did. Ciara still cried and whined although she was getting just a tiny bit better. I had told her that, since Alvin didn't cry in the car, someone might have thought that she was the puppy and not him! She didn't like that idea, so she did try to cry less. Maybe someday she will learn that car rides are good things.

Alvin's first Christmas with us was fun. Mom and Dad decided that we would all go for a ride to look at the holiday lights, just like we did when it was just Duffy and me. Ciara started to whine; but Dad gave her a treat and told her that, if she didn't cry too much, there would be a treat even better than ice cream when we got back home. I was glad it was a colder night because Mom put our fancy coats onto us and then opened the windows so that we could sniff the cold, crisp air. They had Christmas music playing on the car radio, and it even started to snow a little bit. Mom and Dad commented that it truly felt like the holidays had arrived.

After a while, I stretched out and took a nap. As I fell asleep, I could hear the music, hear the quiet murmur of Mom and Dad's conversation, and feel the love surrounding us in the car. Once we got back home, Dad gave us each a special treat of meatballs made from ground lamb. That was so very tasty! Ciara even admitted that a treat like that made the ride almost worthwhile.

In the spring, Mom and Dad did their usual yard cleanup, and I was content to sit in the big yellow chair and rest my head on the arm. From my vantage point, I could watch everyone. Dad raked the dead leaves from the patio while Mom hung her lanterns on nearly every available hook all around the yard. Ciara and Alvin hunted in the woods for chipmunks and mice, and I could hear the chattering of the squirrels in the trees above. The warm sun felt good on my achy hips, and I was thankful that Mom and Dad had decided to bring Alvin home. He was a good companion for Ciara, especially now that I didn't want to play as much.

Once again, we settled into a comfortable routine. Alvin soon learned that he shouldn't try to take over Ciara's spot next to Dad, and I wasn't giving up my spot on the couch with Mom, leaving him the middle of the couch. You see, he was still a little puppy, so he fit there nicely, curled up with his back against Ciara and his head often on my hip. He liked using me as a pillow, and I really didn't mind. We all felt warm and cozy altogether.

Because Alvin was such a young puppy, he still had to sleep in his crate at night. Ciara hated her crate and therefore assumed that Alvin should hate his crate. She did not like it when he had to go into his crate, and she would run at his crate and bark. I tried to explain to her that she was frightening Alvin, but she didn't care. Alvin started to avoid his crate because he didn't like her barking at him. We all had to work at keeping Ciara from upsetting Alvin. I can't say that it always worked, but it eventually got a little bit better.

Somewhere along the line, Ciara moved from Dad's feet to snuggle against his back in the big people bed. She was technically in my spot, but I had pretty much given up my place on the big bed. I couldn't jump up there any longer on my own, and I hated to have to wake someone if I wanted down. I could still jump down on my own, but it hurt my hips and shoulders when I did. Mom bought me a wonderful bed for the floor next to her side of the big bed, so I curled up there at night. Sometimes Mom's hand would hang down, and I could reach it to give her kisses. I am not sure that she really liked it when I kissed her hand while she was sleeping because she usually pulled it away, but it made me feel good to know she was so close.

    We continued to play together, cuddle together, hike together, and go for ice cream together. Life was incredibly good. I know that Mom and Dad still missed Duffy a lot, but Alvin's antics kept them busy. He kept Ciara and me busy too because we tried to teach him proper puppy lessons. He was so stubborn, though, that he often just kept on doing what he wanted. I was very thankful for Ciara a few times when Alvin wanted to tackle me or chase me. She would try to distract him and even stood in front of me so that Alvin would bump her first instead of running into me and knocking me down. She was acting like Alvin's mom dog. Dad called him an Irish hooligan.

Adventures with Alvin

One day, I saw Mom and Dad getting our packs together, and I quickly ran and told Alvin and Ciara. I told them that it looked as though we were going to be going for a hike! While we were all very excited by the idea, Ciara had to complain about the car ride that always went along with our longer hikes. No matter how much she enjoyed the hike, she still had to complain about the car ride.

Meanwhile, I watched as Dad carried their packs out to the car and then came back in for the water jug and our packs. He then went out to the garage and was thumping around out there for a few minutes. He came back through the house carrying some lumpy-looking bags. I wondered what those were all about.

As I watched Mom and Dad putting on their jackets and then checking their pockets for gloves, I remembered that there was snow on the ground. I couldn't remember that we'd ever gone hiking in the snow before, and I was looking forward to trying it. I wondered how different the smells would be.

We all got into the car and settled into our usual spots. I liked to curl up near the very back of the car while Ciara tried to climb into the front seat. Alvin usually stretched out in the middle of the car. I don't think that Ciara wanted to be in the front seat to be with Mom and Dad so much as she wanted to stop the car. I really don't understand why she dislikes car rides as much as she does.

Anyway, we seemed to ride for a long time, much longer than for rides to our usual hiking spots. I could sense a change in elevation as we went up and over a mountain, and that made me wonder even more about where Mom and Dad were taking us.

Finally, Dad pulled into a parking lot, and he and Mom got out. I was startled a bit when they opened the back hatch of the car and then sat down to change their shoes. The boots that they were putting on covered much more of their legs than their usual shoes. Mom then lifted out one of the lumpy bags and pulled out the strangest things I had ever seen. They were bent metal frames with some sort of leathery-looking stuff stretched on the frames. I watched as Mom attached her boot to the middle of the frame and then did the same to her other boot. As she stood up, I realized that she and Dad had the same sort of things on their feet. She reached in and helped me down to the ground, and I immediately had to sniff those weird things from end to end. She laughed a bit and asked me if I liked her snowshoes. Snowshoes? So that was what they were. I guessed that they were to help her walk in the snow, but I really couldn't see how this was going to work.

Mom and Dad chatted a bit while they got their gear together and made sure that we were all securely tethered to them. They reminded us about the rules when they hiked with their hiking poles, and we all listened closely. Well, Ciara and I did. Alvin was too busy running around at the end of his lead, trying to see everything in every direction at once. Dad told him to sit down a few times. Alvin's bottom would briefly touch the ground, and then he'd be up and bouncing around again.

Mom took my lead and Ciara's lead and attached them to her hiking belt. Her hiking belt was a wide belt that had rings for clipping our leads. This way, she could use her poles without having to also hold onto our leads. We just have to remember to stay in front of Mom and in between her poles.

Dad, on the other hand, had decided to hold onto Alvin's leash, in addition to clipping him to the hiking belt. Dad thought this would give him a bit more control over Alvin's wanderings. I seriously doubted that it would work.

Finally, all the preparations were done, and Dad closed the hatch on the car and locked it. We were off!

As we left the parking area, I noticed that Mom and Dad were walking carefully in the tracks left by other hikers. I also figured out that, if I walked where the snow had been pressed down, it was much easier for me and I didn't get as tired. I don't think Alvin even noticed the earlier tracks as he bounded from one side of the pathway to the other.

Unfortunately, I soon started to get really tired, and that upset me. We used to be able to hike for hours, and I wouldn't get tired. This time, we had only walked for about twenty minutes, and I was really beat. I looked back at Mom, and she was talking to Dad as they walked. We only went a little farther when we took a short break for some water. Dad unclipped Alvin's lead from his belt, and Mom unclipped my lead from hers. What was going on? I wondered.

Mom said that she would wait where she was, and Dad said that was a good idea. With that, he hoisted me up onto his shoulders and started to walk back the way we had come. He reassured me that everything was okay but that they could see that I was getting tired, and they didn't want me to get sick or hurt. We were heading back to the car, and he'd see to it that I would be warm and safe in the car while they hiked a bit longer. True to his word, Dad set up a bowl with some water for me and a small bowl with some treats. He also fluffed the blanket that was always in the car, and I was content to curl up for a nap. I was disappointed that I couldn't finish the hike but thankful that I didn't have to. With one more gentle ear rub, Dad closed and locked the car. I sat up and watched as he walked back toward Mom and the others.

I fell asleep and had a truly pleasant dream. During my dream, I relived some of the hikes that Duffy and I had taken, especially the walks on the beach on that first vacation. I also remembered carefully walking out onto the rock for Mom's pictures when we were in Virginia and all of the intriguing smells in the Smoky Mountains. I am sure my toes were twitching as I relived those wonderful adventures.

I don't know how long I had been asleep, but I was suddenly startled awake as the car unlocked and the hatch opened. Alvin leapt into the car, nearly spilling my water bowl. I woofed at him to be careful, but he was too busy checking out my little bowl of treats to listen. Ciara crawled up into the car as well and tried to push Alvin out of the way to get a few treats too, but she was too late. He had cleaned everything out of the bowl.

Dad laughed. He reached into their bags and gave each of us a large cookie. I took mine but didn't start to eat it right away. I was still trying to wake up and was having fun listening to Ciara and Alvin describe their adventure.

They finally settled down and took turns telling me what had happened. I munched on my cookie as I tried to picture the scene. They had gone a distance from where I had turned around and came to a huge meadow. The only tracks in the meadow were along the edges, and Alvin decided that there needed to be some tracks in the middle of the field. Dad had Alvin's lead at that point, and they started out away from the path. Alvin was hopping up and down like a kangaroo because the snow was deeper than his legs. Dad, meanwhile, was sort of floating on top of the snow, only sinking a few inches because of the snowshoes. Since the snow was so deep, they could not see that they were actually on a small hill; and on one of Alvin's hops, he suddenly disappeared into a snowdrift.

Dad reached down to grab the handle on Alvin's harness and fell over into the snowdrift as well. Fortunately he didn't fall on Alvin! Alvin took the opportunity to scramble up onto Dad so that he could see above the snowdrift. Dad struggled a bit and managed to stand up again, but he was no longer floating on the snow. He was standing in a hole in the snow. He picked up Alvin so that he wouldn't jump for a few minutes, and Dad slowly started to walk back toward the trail. He slowly lifted his feet and gradually created a ramp, working his way up to the same level in the snow as the path. This wasn't an easy task, both because of the depth of the snow and because Alvin was wiggling and twisting in Dad's arms. He kept trying to lick Dad's face and his ears, and Dad kept telling Alvin to stop.

Ciara, meanwhile, was sitting on the path with Mom; and she was quite worried. She wanted to run to help Dad, but she was afraid that she'd get stuck in the snow as well. She was very relieved as she watched them get closer and closer and danced in excitement when Dad and Alvin got to where they stood. Mom brushed some of the snow off of Dad's coat and hat and suggested that they head back to the car. Dad agreed and gently set Alvin back down on the path. With that, they started to walk back to the car. Ciara grumbled to Alvin that it was all his fault that the hike had ended, and Alvin retorted that the hike was probably going to end soon anyway because she was complaining that her feet were cold.

I wished that someone had taken a movie of what had happened, but I enjoyed the picture painted by Alvin and Ciara. As their chatter quieted, I listened to Mom and Dad as they relived the afternoon's adventure. Their version was a little different, but the key points were the same as was the conclusion: Alvin was the troublemaker!

Alvin got older and stronger, and at the same time, I found that I was getting tired more quickly and I was feeling achy more frequently. Alvin understood and tried really hard not to hurt me during our games, but sometimes his enthusiasm overpowered his good sense. I don't think he had ever been around an old dog before, and I am not sure he understood why I preferred naps over games of chase. He would learn someday, and Ciara already understood. She started to watch out for me and protect me from Alvin's enthusiasm. In the meantime, I continued taking my naps in sun puddles and chased Alvin in my dreams.

One afternoon, I was slowly making my way along the edge of the woods in our yard, and I really wasn't paying attention to anyone. Ciara looked up from the hole she was digging and saw Alvin preparing to run across the yard and tackle me. I still can't believe that she did it, but she ran full speed from her hole to put herself between the charging Alvin and me! She took the full hit and ended up being knocked over. Alvin stood looking a bit confused; he wasn't expecting to hit Ciara. She turned and gave him a low growl.

"You do not do that to Quincy," she warned.

Alvin stood looking from Ciara to me and then slowly sat down. I kept walking over toward my favorite spot to rest as Ciara sat and faced Alvin.

"Quincy's getting too old for the rough games. He's still the boss of us, but you also have to listen to me. And I'm telling you to not pick on him. You do, and you'll have to answer to me."

Ciara then gave him a stern look as she stood up and walked over to see how I was doing. She told me what she'd said to Alvin and then paused. I thanked her and told her that she had done the right thing.

Alvin came up to us slowly. He flopped down onto the grass, then rolled over onto his back.

He quietly woofed, "I was only playing, Quincy. I would never want to hurt you."

Ciara turned to face him and stared at him intently as she said, "You do, and I will hurt you!"

I assured them both that I was fine and told Alvin that I wasn't upset. I did take advantage of the moment, though, and thank Ciara for defending me and then added, "You are learning the challenges of being senior dog and learning them well. I am confident that Alvin will listen to you once you are senior dog."

Ciara looked at me with a bit of shock in her eyes. "You aren't going anywhere! Not for a long, long time."

I looked away because, this time, I couldn't promise her that was true.

Saying Goodbye

As time went by, I realized that I wasn't having as much fun as before, and I was tired and sore much of the time. I found myself thinking increasingly about Duffy and wondering about life at the Rainbow Bridge. I spent a lot of time thinking about what he told me about the Rainbow Bridge during his visits to me.

As I mentioned before, the Rainbow Bridge is a special place in heaven where dogs wait for their humans to come meet them before going all of the way into heaven. The dogs at the Rainbow Bridge can communicate with their people here on earth by leaving white feathers when they visit. The Rainbow Bridge pups visit when their people are upset or when they need just a bit of special comfort. The dog visitors leave white feathers for their people to find so that they know about the visit and that we all still love each other. Duffy has left a few feathers for Mom and Dad to find, and Mom always has tears in her eyes after she finds one.

Sometimes the pups visit their people in their dreams. Those are really nice because we dogs can run and play with our people like little puppies. Sometimes I think those are harder on the people, though, because they are all happy and excited in their dreams and then they wake up and are sad all over again that their pup is at the Rainbow Bridge.

It's not as difficult for us dogs. The pups at the Rainbow Bridge can visit with earthbound pups more easily, so I'd been talking with Duffy every so often to hear how he was doing since he went to the Rainbow Bridge about two years before. I learned that he was having fun playing with all the other wheatens that were also waiting for their humans. He told me about meeting other wheaten terriers that sort of knew him because their people knew Mom and Dad. He hadn't mentioned meeting any of my brothers or sisters, but I hadn't asked him about them either. Duffy acknowledged that he really missed Mom and Dad but knew that we were taking loving care of them.

During one of my chats with Duffy, I admitted that I was getting awfully tired. Some days, my hips hurt; and other days, they didn't. But I still preferred to sleep much of the day. Or at least I tried to. It seemed as though on the days when I felt most achy and tired were the days that Alvin felt that he should climb on me or pull on my ears. He was only two years old, so I could sort of forgive him, but it wasn't a lot of fun. My nose still worked fine. I could certainly smell cheese from anywhere in the house, but my eyesight was getting dim too. During one of my chats with Duffy, I wondered to him if it was time for me to join him at the Rainbow Bridge. I didn't want to upset Mom and Dad by leaving them. Duffy assured me that Mom and Dad would understand, but I really didn't know how to tell them.

It wasn't too long after my chat with Duffy that Ciara and I had an opportunity to talk. I explained to her that I was getting really tired. It was getting increasingly difficult for me to get up from my bed, and I couldn't see things as clearly as I once could. I also couldn't hear everything as well as before; but I could still smell food and feel love and all those important things.

We could hear Dad roughhousing with Alvin while we talked, and I was glad for that. I didn't want to share some of my thoughts with Alvin just yet. I told Ciara that I'd been talking with Duffy in my dreams and that I thought that the time was coming soon when I'd have to join him. Ciara leaned closely and whimpered a bit. I assured her that I wasn't sick, just getting old. I told her that he had painted a lovely picture of the Rainbow Bridge and that I would come and visit her after I got to the Bridge.

She turned her head slightly and shyly admitted that she and Duffy had been talking too. She knew about my conversations with Duffy, and she agreed that it was time for me to join Duffy at the Rainbow Bridge. None of us knew, though, how to let Mom and

Dad know. We both knew that Mom was going to be the most upset. She called me her heart dog, and she will always be my heart person.

At the same time, Mom and Dad realized that I was getting pretty old for a wheaten terrier; and at fifteen years old, I'd already outlived most of my brothers and sisters from my litter. Mom told me about each one when they transitioned from here to the Bridge, and each time, she cried and hugged me a little tighter. I still didn't know how to tell her, but I knew that I was going to have to transition to the Rainbow Bridge soon. I hoped that Mom and Dad would understand just as Duffy assured me.

Late in the afternoon a few days later, while Mom and Dad were doing their chores around the house, the telephone rang. Mom answered it and then slowly sat down at the dining room table. I could tell by her voice that whatever was being said was upsetting to her, so I sat next to her and rested my head on her leg. I wanted her to know that I was there if she needed a cuddle.

For the longest time, all I heard her say was uh-huh or oh, interspersed by heavy sighs. Dad came over to see what was going on, and Mom motioned for some paper and a pen. I don't know what she wrote, but I could see that whatever it was made Dad sad too.

Mom talked a little while longer and then ended her phone conversation. Mom turned to me and invited me to put my paws up on her leg, and she wrapped her arms around me in a really tight hug. I tried to turn my head to give her kisses, but the way she was holding me prevented me from that.

Dad asked what had happened, and Mom softly explained to Dad that Di had called to tell us that my brother Danny had gone to the Rainbow Bridge. This made me incredibly sad because that meant that Sulley and I were the only ones from my litter still here on earth. I wondered if Duffy had met my siblings since he was already at the Rainbow Bridge.

Mom continued to hug me, and I know that she was thinking about Duffy and all of the other pups that had gone on to the Rainbow Bridge. I know she was also thinking about her friend Di, who now had a wheaten-shaped hole in her heart. I wished we lived closer so that I could give her some cuddles but had to comfort myself with the knowledge that Danny would probably be visiting Di soon and leaving a white feather to let her know that he was still with her in her heart.

That night, Duffy came to me in my dreams, and he told me that he had met Danny. He was pretty sure that they would be good friends, and they had already shared some stories about their lives with me. It felt good to hear about their meeting, but it made me just a little bit sad too. I missed Duffy, and that visit made it particularly hard.

For the next while, Mom gave me extra hugs and cuddles. I'm not sure if they were for me because she thought I needed them or because she needed them herself. It really doesn't matter. Either way, the hugs and ear rubs gave us both some comfort. Meanwhile, Ciara spent her time snuggling with Dad. That really wasn't a change from our normal routine, but I know that Dad was thinking about Duffy and Danny as well.

As it turned out, I didn't have to worry about telling Mom and Dad. Over the period of a few weeks, they had some quiet talks; and then one Saturday morning, she called my veterinarian, Dr. Barbara. I was napping, so I didn't really hear what they talked about. But I did hear Mom say that Dr. Barbara could see me around noon that day. I didn't know what time it was, and I really didn't care. I was snuggling with them on their big bed. This was a special treat for me since I hadn't been able to climb up there with them for a year or two, and I'd nearly forgotten how soft and cozy it was up there. Dad had put an extra blanket under me, so I didn't have to worry about an accident. I was embarrassed by my accidents, but there wasn't much I could do about them. I simply couldn't get up and to the door fast enough anymore.

Dad had put Alvin in his crate, and he was noisily reminding everyone that he was there. He didn't appreciate being left out of whatever was happening. I ignored him and dozed a bit while Mom rubbed my ears. That was so relaxing! Ciara tried to climb up onto the big bed as well, and she was shocked and dismayed when Dad put her back on the floor, explaining that this was time for me to get extra cuddles and love. I'm not sure what shocked Ciara more—that she was told she couldn't be up on the bed or that her Daddy put her on the floor! Dad never said no to Ciara about anything.

But for this time, I was pleased that this was just our time—just me, Mom, and Dad, just like in the beginning. I gave extra licks, and they gave me lots of pets and rubs. I especially loved how Mom was rubbing my ears while Dad massaged my paws. I could feel the love and felt all warm and tingly inside. Mom even stretched out next to me, and I could feel her heart beating against my back. That was extremely comforting, and I think she liked it too.

Mom told me about some of her friends' wheatens who had already gone to the Rainbow Bridge. I knew about many of them because of my talks with Duffy, but it was during one of those stories I realized that I wasn't going to have to tell her that it was time for me to join them there because she already knew. My heart swelled with even more love because I knew Mom and Dad loved me enough to let me leave and join Duffy.

Mom buried her face in my neck and started to cry. I could feel how sad she was, and I knew that we would all miss one another. I turned and licked away her tears one more time. She hugged me tightly and said that I truly was her heart dog and that she would hold me deep in her heart forever. I licked her nose and promised her the same.

Dad brought a small bowl to me, and it was filled with shredded cheese! Cheese was always my favorite treat, and it was nice to have this all to myself. I savored each bit and then rested my head on Mom's leg for a brief nap.

While I was napping, I had the most wonderful dream! It was sort of a movie, showing me the best moments of my entire life. I was reminded of the time I stole the green Christmas cookies during Mom's basket party. I laughed in my dream when Dad called Mom and asked, "What did you do to my dog?" I had pooped green poop as a result of the green cookies.

I remembered standing on the wall along the Skyline Drive in Virginia. It was beautiful looking out over the trees and valleys, and I could tell that Mom and Dad loved that place too. That scene then reminded me of the time that Duffy and I got to go with them to the

Smoky Mountains too. That trip was awesome. I'm glad that we only smelled the bears and the moose.

I thought back to our first trip to the beach and meeting up with my brother Sulley on our way home. I also thought about the time I met my sister Molly June at the dog convention. I knew Molly June was at the Rainbow Bridge and looked forward to seeing her there, along with the others.

I thought about running through the snow at home, pushing my nose like a snowplow and getting covered with little snowballs that stuck to my hair. I smiled at the memory of our Christmas Eve car rides to look at the lights. Mom and Dad always had a mug of hot chocolate for themselves and extra-special treats for Duffy and me.

I remembered how Ciara and I comforted each other after Duffy died and how together we helped Mom and Dad feel a little bit better. I chuckled when I remembered how Ciara protected me from the rambunctious puppy that was Alvin.

I thought about all of our friends, people that I had grown to love through the years, and how fortunate I was to be part of such a loving group of people. I was happy to know that I had helped introduce Mom and Dad to so many wonderful wheaten people from all over the world. I was still smiling in my dream when Dad came in and told us that we had some friends that had stopped by to see me.

Dad lifted me down from the bed, and we went out to the living room. I walked slowly over to my soft big bed, and I was lying there on my fluffy big bed when the front door opened. It was our special friends Katie and Dee. They seemed sad, but they were trying to hide those emotions from me. I started to get up to greet them, but Katie told me to stay where I was. She came over and knelt on the floor next to me. She gently rubbed my ears and then she leaned forward to me and gave me an extra-special kiss. She whispered in my ear that I was the best wheaten terrier she had ever known and that she was extremely glad that she had been able to love me. I wagged my tail at her words and gave her kisses all over her hand. I remembered that she didn't like licks on her face, and I was determined to be a good boy this time. Katie surprised by hugging me, and I couldn't help myself. I had to kiss her cheek one last time. She kissed my nose and said that it was okay.

I noticed that Dee had moved closer to us, so I sat up to make it easier for Dee to pet me. I knew that she wasn't a dog lover, so I felt extra honored that she wanted to see me and to pet me. I gave her an ever-so-gentle little kiss on her hand to say thank you. She smiled a shy smile and patted my head again.

After a little while, Katie said that they had to leave. She said that they had some errands to run, but I think she didn't want me to see her tears. A few more kisses and they were on their way, but not before Katie whispered to me to tell Duffy that she missed him. I wagged my tail to tell her that I would do that. With that, Dee and Katie quietly left. I could hear their sniffles and knew that they would miss me as much as I would miss them. I was thankful that Mom and Dad had such good friends, and I made a mental note to myself to ask Duffy if we were allowed to visit friends from the Rainbow Bridge or if our visits could only be to family. I certainly hoped that I could visit friends. As I mulled over that question, I looked up over the fireplace and saw the gifts Mom and Dad received after Duffy died. I felt comforted because I knew that their friends would support them after I went to the Rainbow Bridge too.

After they left, Mom brought me a cheeseburger! I ate a bit of it, but to be honest, I really wasn't interested in eating much. I felt a little sad because I knew Mom had made the cheeseburger just for me as a special treat, but I knew she would understand. She would share it with Alvin and Ciara later, I hoped. I rested my head on a pillow to take a brief rest.

Mom looked at her watch and quietly said to Dad, "It's time."

Dad went to get my leash, and both Ciara and Alvin ran to the door. We usually traveled as a pack, so they were both a bit confused when Dad told them to back up away from the door. I woofed quietly to Ciara that I would miss her but I'd tell Duffy that she was doing well. Ciara wagged her tail a little. I know she hated to admit it, but she missed having Duffy around to tease. She understood what I was trying to say and gave me some extra kisses, whispering that I should "share some of those with Duffy. I really do still miss him." I assured her that I would.

I also asked Ciara to explain the Rainbow Bridge to Alvin. He didn't know any pups who had made that transition yet, so he hadn't learned about it. Duffy didn't visit Alvin when he came because Alvin joined our pack after Duffy left. Ciara told me that she would so that he would be prepared for my visit.

I went over to Alvin and touched noses with him. He looked between me and Ciara with a very confused look on his face. I told Alvin that I was going to go see Dr. Barbara and that I wouldn't be coming home ever again. He clearly didn't understand, and Ciara's quiet whimpers didn't help him at all. We touched noses again. We shared some kisses, and Ciara promised to give Mom and Dad extra snuggles and kisses. With that, I walked with Mom and Dad out to the front yard.

We walked out of the house slowly, and I paused on the front sidewalk. I took a couple of deep breaths trying to commit the comforting smells of home into my memory. After a few more steps toward the car, I paused, and Dad helped me up into the car. It had been getting harder and harder for me to climb up into the car by myself, and I was happy to accept his help. I still loved riding in the car, though, with the rush of wind in my hair and my ears flopping in the breeze. Unfortunately, it was pretty cold outside, so I doubted that Dad would put the windows down for this trip.

Mom sat in the back seat with me. This was unusual. She always sat up front with Dad, but I was glad that she was there. I was just a little bit nervous about what was going to happen, so I licked her leg to try to calm myself. Ordinarily she would have been a little annoyed that I was getting her pant leg all wet, but she didn't seem to mind this time. She simply rested her hand on my back, and I could feel her gently tracing the scar from that injury so long ago.

"I thought we were going to lose you then, Quincy," she murmured. "I'm so thankful that we didn't."

I thought back to when I was around three years old and I got hurt so badly that they had to rush me to the dog emergency room. That was a long time ago, but my wound was so deep that

Mom could still feel it. Even though it hurt back then and the whole episode was scary, it was comforting to think back on how well Mom and Dad took care of me, just like they were taking care of me now.

While Dad drove, I rested my head on Mom's leg, and she gently rubbed my ears.

"I'm going to miss you, Quincy. You are my most favorite wheaten in the world," she said, barely holding back tears.

She bent down to hug me, and I gently licked away those tears. That had been my job from the time I was a little puppy, and I was just a little bit sad that this would probably be the last time I could try to help her feel better. I knew Ciara could do it and hoped that Alvin would learn to comfort Mom and Dad as well, but that had been my job for so long. I would need to remember when I visited Ciara to tell her that was one of her new responsibilities.

I shifted my position to sit up and look out of the window. Dad surprised me by opening the window, and the frigid air filled the car. I put my nose up and sniffed all the wonderful smells coming in and thought about my whole life that was filled with good things. I also realized that we were not taking our usual route to Dr. Barbara's office. Dad was taking some country roads that curved and turned and went up and down hills. I think he was trying to make the trip last just a little longer, and I enjoyed the extra things to sniff. I looked up at Mom, though, and she looked cold! I snuggled back down on the seat to let Dad know he could close the window again.

After a bit, Dad turned into the parking lot for Dr. Barbara's office and rolled up the window. We all got out of the car slowly, and while Dad walked me over to the side for the usual potty stop, Mom went inside to tell them that we were at the office. We stood around outside while we waited for our turn to go in. After a short wait, Brooke came to the door and told us that we could come inside.

As we walked into Dr. Barbara's office, I tried to stand up tall and walk as well as I could. I wanted everyone to remember me as a strong and healthy pup, not an old dog. The staff all greeted me like an old friend, and I returned their greetings. I had known many of them after all for fifteen years—my entire life. I walked slowly into the exam room and started my usual tour of the room, smelling all of the smells.

One of the technicians brought a couple of blankets in and spread them on the floor. After I checked out the entire room, I was more than happy to take a rest in the middle of the soft purple blanket.

Mom chuckled a bit and said, "Royal purple for a prince of a dog."

Again I rested my head on her leg and started licking her hand. While I was resting, several of the office staff came in and gave me a few pets and offered treats. As usual, I took their treats to be polite but set them down on the blanket after they left. I did the same thing when I was younger. Mom always said that I was very fussy about my treats.

After a little while, Dr. Barbara came in, and she bent low to talk with me a little bit. She seemed sad too. I gave her hands a few kisses to let her know that I appreciated the diligent care she had given me through the years. She stood up and chatted with Mom and Dad for a few minutes and agreed that they were doing the right thing. She said that one of the technicians would be in within a few minutes to give me some medicine to help me relax, and she left to deal with some other business.

I napped a little bit while we waited, so I was a little startled when my favorite technician touched me gently. She rubbed my neck and talked to me quietly. I honestly didn't feel her give me the medicine. She stood up and asked another technician to come in. Together they lifted me gently up onto the table using the purple blanket.

Dad came over and gave me some hugs and kisses, and I gave a few lazy kisses back. I was really sleepy, but I was trying to stay awake to see what would happen next. He bent slightly and looked deep into my eyes. He wrapped his arms around me, burying his face in my neck and inhaled deeply, trying to memorize my smells. I didn't know that people could smell that well!

Mom pulled a chair over and put her nose next to mine and started rubbing my ears. That felt so good! I gave her a few kisses as she kissed my nose. I hadn't noticed Dr. Barbara come back into the room, and she gave me some more medicine. I drifted off to sleep feeling the love surround me. The last thing I felt was Mom kissing my nose.

Even as I fell asleep, I could sense everyone's love, and I thought about what a lucky pup I was—I had never wanted for food, shelter, warmth, or comfort. I had a great life filled with love and wonderful people.

I didn't see Mom and Dad leave Dr. Barbara's office, but I know that it had to have been hard for them to walk out carrying only my collar. It had to be equally hard for them to go home and have only Ciara and Alvin there, but I knew that those two would help ease the pain. I was just really glad that Mom and Dad had been strong enough to keep their promise. They thought of me and made sure that I didn't hurt and that I could keep my dignity. They were excellent dog parents.

Meanwhile, I knew that I wasn't still at Dr. Barbara's office in my old and tired body because I could look around and see everything clearly and I didn't hurt anymore. I could also see a huge banner welcoming me to the Rainbow Bridge. I had heard stories about the Rainbow Bridge. Now I could find out what it was really like. While I was still a little sad leaving Mom and Dad, I was looking forward to this new adventure. Suddenly I heard some excited barking, and I looked up to see Duffy running toward me! What adventures did he have planned?

Duffy came charging toward me and nearly skidded into a pile of leaves next to me. He always was a bit clumsy!

"Welcome to the Rainbow Bridge!" he woofed.

He went on to tell me that I would soon discover that there were mountains of stuffed toys, pillows, and treats everywhere. The planner angels take care of everything down to the smallest detail. We walked together, with Duffy gently leading me to my new home. Once there, Duffy showed me my welcome bag. I looked into it and discovered that it even had a Kitty that was exactly like my favorite toy at home. There were also chunks of my favorite cheeses and a few peanut butter snacks. I looked around my room and realized that it had the TV room back at home, down to the last detail, including my bed with my name embroidered on it. The only things missing were Mom and Dad.

Before I could dwell on that, my eyes fell onto another special sight—a second bed and a squishy ball bed that we used to have in our TV room. Sitting on that bed was my brother Duffy! He was grinning from ear to ear, and his tail was wagging as hard as it ever had. He confirmed for me that we would be sharing a room at the Bridge just as we had back on earth.

Duffy told me about some new arrival lessons that I needed to pay attention to. I would learn about long-distance comforting and how to leave evidence of our visits. This sounded intriguing, so I asked where I would go to sign up. Duffy laughed and said that I already knew! I looked at him with a puzzled look; and he explained that, when we came across the first bridge, we automatically knew those lessons. I stopped for a minute and realized it was true. I already knew how to leave a feather for Mom to find to let her know that I was safe because I had already left one on her desk at home. I wondered when she would find it and hoped that she would know that it came from me.

I asked Duffy who had shown him around when he first arrived because I knew that he didn't have anyone else from our family already here.

Duffy smiled and said, "Remember Mom's friend Sherry? Remember them talking about Bailey?"

It turns out that Bailey met Duffy and showed him how things worked. They had become the best of buddies, and Duffy couldn't wait for me to meet him. I told him that Mike and Sherry were the pet parents of my brother Sulley! What a wonderfully small world.

While I was looking forward to meeting Bailey, I had some other important meetings to attend. I asked Duffy to show me the communication center, so we walked over together. I could tell that he was excited to see me because he kept bumping my shoulder to knock me off of the walking path, just as he had back when we hiked together with Mom and Dad. It was after one of those pushes that I realized that I didn't have any more aches or pains. I could also see as clearly as I could as a puppy. I was really happy about that.

We arrived at the communication center; and I left a message for my dog mom, Morgan, and my puppy siblings Whiskey, Danny, Sophie, Murphy, and Molly June. Within minutes, Duffy found himself swallowed up in a happy pile of wheaten terriers, and we all greeted each other with many sniffs and licks. I introduced Duffy to everyone, and we wandered over to a quiet spot to catch up. As to be expected, Whiskey ran ahead to find the perfect spot, and Molly June stopped by one of the many treat stations along the way. Some things never change!

Duffy sat back and listened to us as we caught up on each other's lives.

Murphy told us that he was proudest of his cousin's accomplishments in lure coursing. "Mochi can chase that flag faster than anyone...and it's all because I taught him how!" he bragged.

We asked Murphy about his own ribbons from competing, and he hesitated a little bit before answering. His sister Reilly had joined our group by now, and before he could answer, she proudly told us about the quilt that Pat had made from all of Murphy's ribbons. Murphy looked both pleased and embarrassed as we all congratulated him.

Danny was next to chime in. He told us that he had gotten hurt in an accident and he started to have a lot of trouble walking. He loved Diane and Rob, but he was having such a challenging time getting around that he wasn't able to have much fun. He got to meet his sister Maryann before coming to the Rainbow Bridge, and he was glad that she was with Di to keep her company. Maryann is a show dog, just like Sophie, so she is keeping Di busy. Danny went on to tell us that he was thankful that his mom realized that it was time for him to come to the Bridge.

Whiskey had a wonderful life with Jeanne. He described how much he loved his human friend Patti and how sad everyone was when had gotten sick when he was still pretty young. The doctors were astounded with the care that Jeanne gave him and what a good boy he was on each doctor's visit. He was proud to tell us all that he had contributed to the health information for our breed. We all thought that it was just like Whiskey to find the good news in something that could be really sad. Whiskey assured us that everything was fine. He also told us about his brother still back on earth. Sprocket was keeping Jeanne company although Sprocket hadn't mastered the art of stealing sandwiches. Whiskey's only regret was that he hadn't passed those lessons along before he came to the Rainbow Bridge. Someone commented that, among our group, Whiskey had been at the Bridge the longest.

"Well, not quite the longest," chimed in Molly June. She pointed to her brother Buddy, who was wandering around wearing his trademark necktie. "Buddy is the mayor here, just like he was at home in Delaware," she proudly explained.

We didn't correct Molly that Buddy hadn't been part of our group because we knew that she was so proud of Buddy that she needed to point him out to us. Molly June went on to tell us that she had had an important job before she left earth. She was responsible for helping her people, Denise and Jim, take in senior wheaten terriers and give them all the love and happiness that they could. She commented that it was always really hard on Denise when it came time for one of the pups to come to the Rainbow Bridge, but she and Jim always put the pups first.

Molly looked around for a moment and said, "There are a lot of my family here, Plushy, Sunny, Buddy, and Charles. We fill a whole section at dinner!"

Sophie was sitting quietly, and I asked her how life in California had been. She looked down shyly and said that it had been a lot of fun. She had a younger brother, Winston, that she played with; and some of Winston's brothers and sisters would come over to their house to play sometimes. With a little prodding, Sophie also mentioned that she had done quite well in her show career, earning the title of grand champion. We were all so proud of her.

I moved over to sit with Sophie. It felt so good to sit next to her just like we did before she moved to California with Conrad and Laura. We didn't say much to each other; we didn't have to. We still had that special bond that we had shared as little puppies. Sophie did say that she was glad that her people had gotten a new girl puppy, Whitney, to keep her brother Winston company. She then got a faraway look in her eyes, and I knew that she was dropping in for a little visit with her family on earth. They would find a white feather sometime later that evening.

It had taken Morgan a little while to make her way to where we were all sitting. She said that she could hear our laughter from the other side of the field. She was excited to meet Duffy and welcomed him with a friendly hug. She followed Molly June's gaze as she pointed out her family. Morgan was impressed to see Buddy's necktie. Though she had heard the stories before, she listened attentively as we all recounted our lives. She beamed with pride as she heard about our accomplishments.

During a lull in the conversation, I asked Morgan, "And what about you? How has your life been?"

Morgan chuckled and then told us about her life. She started by telling us that, after we all left, things were noticeably quiet at Cam's house. They both enjoyed the calm, but there was a little sadness as Cam put away all of our puppy things. Morgan had made sure that she snuck a couple of the toys into her crate and bed because they had our smells on them and she could sniff them and think of us. She did this quite often.

Morgan then surprised us when she told us that Cam had gotten another wheaten terrier after we all left. Gracie wasn't a young puppy, but rather she was about three years old when she came to live with Cam and Morgan. At first, Morgan wasn't happy that there was another girl in the family; but over time, she and Gracie had become the best of friends.

A few months later, Cam surprised Morgan when she brought out all of the puppy stuff again; Morgan knew she wasn't having puppies. That was when she realized she was going to be an auntie as Gracie was getting ready to have pups. Morgan spent quite a bit of time explaining to Gracie what was going to happen and what she would be doing and promising to help her with the puppies. Gracie was thankful for the help, and together they all waited for the pups to arrive.

Everything went well, and soon there were three puppies getting into everything. Like our litter, each puppy had a distinct personality and kept both Morgan and Gracie busy trying to keep them out of trouble. Chewy loved destroying toys. Dallas liked sports and reminded Morgan a little bit of Murphy, and Sprocket kept everyone on their toes!

Whiskey perked up his ears when Morgan said Sprocket.

Morgan laughed and nodded. "Yes, the very same Sprocket that you tried to teach sandwich stealing."

Whiskey grinned when he realized that Sprocket knew Morgan. He commented that he would have to talk to Sprocket about that during one of his visits.

Morgan said that, as much as she loved the puppies and was proud of Gracie for how she raised them, she was relieved when they went to their forever homes. Chewy went to Melanie and Paul in Pennsylvania and quickly learned their routines of work and school plays. Chewy liked to go to rehearsals periodically, and the schoolkids loved having him there. Dallas went to another family in New Jersey and loved being an only pup. She was happiest when she joined her mom at the baseball park. She was even featured during the local TV news program when they attended an event. Dallas looked quite cute wearing her baseball jersey.

Sprocket learned to open the back door and kept his mom, Jeanne, busy as he would sneak out and dig in the flower beds every chance that he got. With the puppies in their new homes, it was quiet again at Cam's house, and that was what Morgan liked best. Cam had decided that she was going to wait a while before arranging for Gracie to have more puppies, and the three of them enjoyed that quiet time together.

After a couple more years passed, Morgan said that she knew it was time to come to the Rainbow Bridge because she was very tired. She didn't think that she was sick, but she didn't feel like doing much of anything. One afternoon, she crawled onto her bed and went to sleep. Cam was extremely upset when Morgan didn't wake up but recognized that Morgan was free from any pain. We all nodded and understood both the relief we all felt here at the Rainbow Bridge, but we also recognized that our people would be sad and that they would miss us.

New Friends and Feathers

I've been at the Rainbow Bridge now for a little over a year now. I have met lots of new wheaten terrier friends, and we have fun together. It is so peaceful here, and there never are any fights or growls. We all get along, and there is plenty of everything for all of us.

We all stay busy, and our days are filled with our favorite things. Some of the group love the water, and they are always in the pool swimming. Murphy has been giving lure-coursing lessons to anyone who is interested. He is a natural teacher, even if he can be a bit grumpy and stern.

Molly June is the official treat-station greeter. She makes sure that everyone knows where all the treats are. I think she's most excited because she can have all the treats she can possibly want but she never gains an ounce! It is fun to watch the new arrivals as they walk around with her, and she points out every location. They're always surprised when the treat stations have their particular favorites. I don't know how that works, but I never get a treat that I don't like. I was at one of the treat stations recently and got a delicious peanut butter treat, and the pup behind me received a liver treat. How the treat station knew that I didn't like liver baffles me.

Danny, Whiskey, and Duffy have become great friends. They play endless games of chase and then collapse for naps in the sunshine. I love the pure happiness on their faces and enjoy their silly antics. It is good that there is an endless supply of balls and tug toys for them to destroy. Even better though are the evenings when Duffy and I settle into our room and tell stories of our lives on earth or look in on Mom and Dad. We laugh together as we watch Alvin's antics.

I've also met pups from other friends of Mom and Dad. Tagalong is a black schnauzer, and he towers over me. He is a bit headstrong but still a really nice pup. His family includes Bailey and Bentley. Bailey is just about the smallest shih tzu that I've ever seen. I helped introduce her to Molly June, and they can often be seen discussing which treats are the best. Bentley will sometimes join Duffy and Danny in their ball games. He runs as fast as he can trying to keep up with them, but his little shih tzu legs really are no match for my brothers.

Henry and AJ are huge greyhounds! I met Henry on earth when I was a young pup, along with his Chihuahua brother, Igor. Henry has other family here, including some bunnies, rats, and a bearded dragon. Everyone gets along, and there are never any quarrels. It has been interesting getting to know some of these other critters!

I still enjoy the company of my siblings best, and Sophie and I can usually be found sitting on the hill and just watching everyone. We sometimes take walks together and talk about our people, and we laugh at what's going on around us. Sometimes we are joined by another Riley. That Riley was the pup of Mom and Dad's friends in Pennsylvania. Conversations are always quite philosophical when he's with us. Sophie calls me the professor, just like Mom and Dad did, and she has nicknamed Riley the theologian. I will admit that we have some interesting conversations!

One of the best things about being here at the Rainbow Bridge is that we can see our people who are still back on earth. We are allowed to visit them, and we can leave special messages for them. As I mentioned before, the most common message is a white feather. Nearly everyone recognizes that as a sign that we've come to visit. In fact, we are asked to send a feather as soon as we arrive. I left mine for Mom and Dad to find even before I got to my room here. I was excited to see that Mom put my first feather in the memory box that she had made with my collar, my tags, and a snippet of my hair. She had made a similar shadow box for Duffy, and his first feathers are in there as well.

I learned that we could visit other people as well. I was really glad to hear that, so one of my first nonfamily visits was to Katie. On my first visit, I left a feather for her on her nightstand; but I think her cat, Smudge, took it to play with.

Sometimes we visit our people, and we don't leave a feather. I'd done that a couple of times when I could see that Mom was especially sad. I would wait for her to go to sleep, and then I'd gently snuggle with her. She could see me in her dreams, and she could feel my heart beating with hers. I always try to sneak in a few kisses during those visits, and she usually feels better the next day. Sometimes it takes a visit from both Duffy and me to help.

Duffy makes regular visits too, and unbelievably he often talks to Ciara. He is trying to teach her how to best comfort Dad. Duffy and Dad had a special bond, and Ciara does too. Ciara's just a little too self-centered to be quite as good as Duffy at giving comfort, but please don't tell her that I said that.

I feel incredibly lucky to have had such a good life on earth with such great parents. Both of my brothers, Duffy and Alvin, were great brothers; and Ciara is a wonderful sister. While I miss not being able to snuggle with everyone, I know that they are content because I can see them as I watch over them. They also know that I'm doing fine because I leave a feather every so often. Truthfully Duffy and I usually visit at the same time, so they often find two feathers!

Well, I'm going to go find Sophie and see if she wants to go nap in a sun puddle in the meadow. I love just smelling the warm spring smells and letting a nap slowly take over as we lean together. That is certainly a wonderful way to fill an afternoon.

Author's Note

If Quincy's story has inspired you to add a wheaten to your world, may I respectfully suggest checking the Soft Coated Wheaten Terrier Club of America's website (www.scwtca.org). I also would recommend checking with the wheaten rescues listed on that site.

If not a wheaten, I will refrain from asking why not but will still respectfully suggest you check with a reputable rescue or breeder for your new companion. Please do the research—let's work together to shut down the puppy mills.

About the Illustrator

Wendy Carty spent a number of years moving around the country before settling in Connecticut with her husband and their two children. As she was always doodling, her artistic talent led her to creating a Facebook cartoon chronicling the escapades of her Airedale terrier, Pixie. An Irish terrier, Tod, now provides inspiration for her drawings; and she incorporates that indomitable terrier spirit in her very popular artwork. Wendy also lends her talents to several philanthropic organizations that aid fellow terrier owners.

About the Author

Diane McHutchison is an IT person by day and a stained-glass artist, weaver, watercolorist, and author by night. She lives in New Jersey with her husband, John, and two wheatens, Ciara and Aoidhghean. They first met the wheaten terrier breed through friends who were owned by Erin, a lovely wheaten with impeccable manners and a gentle spirit. When Erin's dog sitter learned of a wheaten puppy needing a new home, the sitter spoke with Erin's mom, who, in turn, talked to Diane. A few days later, Quincy, his comfy bed with his name embroidered on the top, and his favorite toy Kitty came to live with Diane and John. As in the story, Duffy came from a shelter, and they suspect some of his quirks came from being taken from his mom so early in life. Ciara (Kitty) was indeed a rescue and has John wrapped around her paw. After Duffy died, they made the conscious decision to get Aoidhghean from a reputable breeder, knowing that his parents would have been chosen to improve the breed's health, temperament, and conformation.

CPSIA information can be obtained
at www.ICGtesting.com
Printed in the USA
BVHW082029190223
658756BV00003B/544